LUCKY

Lesley Ann Eden

MAPLE
PUBLISHERS

Lucky 2 Love

Author: Lesley Ann Eden

Copyright © Lesley Ann Eden (2024)

The right of Lesley Ann Eden to be identified as author of this work has been asserted by the author in accordance with section 77 and 78 of the Copyright, Designs and Patents Act 1988.

First Published in 2024

ISBN 978-1-83538-084-0 (Paperback)
     978-1-83538-085-7 (Hardback)
     978-1-83538-086-4 (E-Book)

Cover design adapted from a painting by S.J.Jameson. Witches Stitch.

Book layout by:
     White Magic Studios
     www.whitemagicstudios.co.uk

Published by:
     Maple Publishers
     Fairbourne Drive, Atterbury,
     Milton Keynes,
     MK10 9RG, UK
     www.maplepublishers.com

LOVE IS ALL YOU NEED.......

John Lennon

CONTENTS

INTRODUCTION

THERE IS NO DEATH! 5

THERE IS NO TIME BEYOND TIME 15

THINK LUCKY AND YOU WILL BE LUCKY 22

TECHNO-MANIA.. 32

MIND OVER MATTER.. 45

REBIRTHING vs REGENERATION... 55

XIAN ZU TRAINING 72

FORWARDS, BACKWARDS TO THE PRESENT 90

MARTA...108

BUILDING BRIDGES FOR TOMORROW............................119

WHEN YOU'RE NOT LOOKING BUT SEEING SIDEWAYS – YOU SEE
THE WORLD AS IT REALLY IS! 129

HOLES IN MAPS LEAD TO SOMEWHERE! 147

PUPPY LOVE 159

GOING BACK 172

TOMORROW AND TOMORROW AND.................................185

THERE IS NO END – ONLY NEW BEGINNINGS.................192

INTRODUCTION
THERE IS NO DEATH!

A Conversation with the late Dr Wayne Dyer

There is no 'death'; only a discarding of a corporal body. Death should not be feared but revered as a natural positive process, rather than a cessation of existence. The physical procedure of death is as easy as stepping outside your front door to begin a new adventure and the transition from your physical form to non-physical, is as natural as breathing, for you have done it many times!

You are born to die. On entering mortality you accept the terms and conditions dictating your human state and whether the termination of your contract is through illness, a fatal accident, a brutal assault, or a heart attack, the procedure provides your doorway to a realm beyond the beyond, where you return to your spiritual home.

The process towards the final exit can for some, be painful, stressful, confusing and terrifying. In other cases it is painless, calming and accepted like drifting into a deep sleep. No matter the condition in which you exit life, there is one thing for certain - there is only a physical separation of your body from the real 'you'. Your 'essence' your 'spirit energy' can never die or fade away, for it is like electricity which vibrates through the cosmos. It is eternal. When darkness descends internally in our minds and our consciousness is clouded by fear and uncertainty, the greatest protection and source of comfort to guide us through distraught times is the knowledge that you are not your body; you are not your brain; you are not your mind; you are all pure spirit energy that can never die.

I know this for certain and can categorically state that 'life after death' exists and is a stronger force than life in the present as I have had countless conversations with people who have moved on from their earthly existence, providing concrete evidence to their loved ones and proving that there is no death.

I would like to share three cases in particular, where psionic contact with the deceased made a tremendous difference to their loved ones. The first case was a lawyer whose wife died after a long illness whom I met, when I was visiting a friend. He was distraught and lost in a deep depression. He didn't believe in the 'afterlife' and was inconsolable at the thought that he would never see his beloved wife again. As he poured out his grief, I was looking out of a window into a lovely garden, when I heard a woman's voice speaking clearly in my head. She said she was the man's wife and asked me to tell her grieving husband that she was fine. Sometimes it is a little awkward, in cases where the deceased asks me to speak on their behalf, especially if the loved one refuses to believe in life after death. But I never refuse a request, even at the cost of being ridiculed. I relayed the message to him and he scorned my words, thinking I had made up the message to make him feel better. Then the voice spoke again and said:

"Ask him about the green socks, it was a secret code we had together. No one else knew about it!"

It seemed a very strange request, but I always did my best to pass on messages, however absurd. So I asked him about the 'green socks'. He went white and sat down and asked me to repeat the message. I relayed it word for word and he burst into tears, as only he knew the significance of the special code they had devised together. He explained it was a secret expression they had used as a code to describe a person with radical, left-wing opinions and they would smile and say to each other, ...'he/she is wearing green socks!'

I had no previous knowledge of him or his wife and certainly no idea about the 'green socks' code, so it was proof to him that she still existed in spirit and he changed his mind about the 'afterlife' as the experience gave him comfort and support to face the future. Many people have drawn deep solace from knowing their loved ones exist beyond the grave, giving a wonderful surety that life is more than a body.

The second case I want to share was particularly special. It involved five daughters who lost their mother, very suddenly and unexpectedly. I had been asked to do a psionic contact by a friend who trusted and believed in my gift, because she knew how upset and inconsolable the sisters were at losing their mother in such tragic circumstances.

It was a Friday evening. I was tired after a long working week and didn't feel I had enough inner energy to face the task. I wanted to cancel the meeting, but I was persuaded by my friend to go and meet the sisters. When I reluctantly arrived at their house they were sitting in a semi-circle, waiting for me. I apologised profusely explaining that I really didn't feel up to the session and I was worried that communication might not happen. However, as soon as I uttered the words a rustling, whistling sound surged through my ears and the deceased mother came through enthusiastically, determined to communicate with her daughters. She was a strong, forceful person who never took no for an answer in life - her presence was powerful!

She began by admonishing her eldest daughter who was sitting next to me, for displaying a disdainful, negative, antagonistic attitude towards me. She berated her for not believing in the afterlife and for being blatantly rude. The eldest daughter was shocked by her mother's out- burst but it was the truth, for she had openly displayed her distrust and dislike of me and being reproved by her mother, she was ashamed and burst into tears recognising the truth of her mother's words. She was most apologetic and after the initial shock of their mother's anger, the other daughters each waited for her to address them. She gave them all unique proof of her identity and expressed her deep sadness at having left them all so abruptly. At the end of the session all the daughters were convinced of their mother's presence and were comforted and assured that she lived on and would be watching over them.

At the end of the session their mother apologised to me for taking over so quickly but she was relieved to find a reliable channel through which to communicate with her daughters. The amazing thing was that instead of draining me, that session filled me with wonderful warmth and positive energy.

The third experience I want to share was a very sad case of an elderly couple who had lost both their sons in a car accident. I knew nothing of their family as I had never met them before and was recommended to them by another client who had a wonderful experience when I contacted her deceased son. The wife of the bereaved couple was very open to accepting life after death but her husband was sceptical and only agreed to accompany his wife to the meeting in the hope it might appease her anguish. I did not know the reason for their visit. I preferred not to have any previous knowledge of a client.

As soon as we sat down around my table, I closed my eyes and heard the sound of a great gushing wind whooshing in my ears and then - their two sons stood before me. I could see a crash in my mind like a video playing and the eldest son spoke:

"One minute we were here and the next we were on another plane, but we were together."

As he spoke I saw the accident. I watched the sons drive a white van over a tiny, brick bridge crashing head on into a large lorry. The younger son added:

"Honestly Mum, there was no pain. We felt nothing!"

The elderly couple exchanged loving glances. The eldest son expressed great sadness at not being able to attend his daughter's birthday party explaining how he had watched it all from afar, describing the events in detail. His surprised parents were in tears at the accuracy of his descriptions and the communication. Both sons relayed private messages to their parents, who were convinced beyond any doubt, of the authenticity of the experience.

Finally both sons thanked them for planting a commemorative tree in their garden to celebrate their lives. They even described where the tree was situated and the landscape around it. The couple were tremendously moved by the whole encounter and went away feeling comforted and reassured that their sons lived on in another realm.

The body you adopt when you enter earth is a vehicle which transports you through life and once discarded, the inner energy naturally seeks the plane from whence you came. You adopt human form for the duration of your visit to earth and when you depart you return to your original source. In taking human form you agree to the rules of entrance- which means you are not allowed to remember who you are, or where you came from, because it is part of the 'life game' to find your true self through the daily quagmire of living.

Once you dare to seek the secrets of the universe, your understanding of who you are, where you came from and to where you will return, becomes clearer. In knowing ourselves we become closer to our spirit source. Cellular death of the body ends the physical journey but inner energy lives on to seek further enlightenment and knowledge of our true spirit essence. What awaits after stepping out of your body is different for everyone, as each individual spirit resonates at a unique frequency and depending on the strength and power of the chi-(soul energy) the soul will find its own exclusive level.

This was verified for me from the wonderful, inspirational Dr Wayne Dyer after his passing. I know this is difficult to accept, but death is only a stripping away of all that is not you. Your body is a vehicle, a container housing and transporting your soul energy through a journey which you have mapped out for yourself, to advance spiritually.

Eckhart Tolle states that 'the secret of life is to die before you die and find that there is no death'. Similarly, Carlos Castaneda suggests that we live our lives like Warriors equipped to die at any moment, having prepared a special place in our minds to go to when we leave our bodies and taking each day as our last. David Icke states that dying is only a transference of attention from one reality to another and that leaving is a natural process. Scientists such as Stuart Hameroff from Arizona University and Sir Roger Penrose from England have explored the concept of quantifying the soul. They believe that there is a Quantum Code which can re-install life after death by triggering a code stored at a Quantum level within our DNA. They believe that this soul energy can never die - rather it traverses to another sphere and through their research, they believe, without doubt, that there is no death. Similarly, Dr Rauni Luukanen Kilde who wrote and lectured on parapsychology, ufology and mind control, states unconditionally that 'there is no death' and recalls countless experiences to prove her theory.

Currently, scientists are researching the idea that death does not exist because life simply takes on another form, at the point of bodily malfunction. The biocentric theory of the universe, which postulates that consciousness creates reality, therefore time and death do not exist because consciousness is, has been and always will be and to that end, death is not possible. Einstein and his colleague John Wheeler, agreed that time is not a fundamental aspect of reality and that only a series of 'eternal nows' are real. The neurosurgeon Eben Alexander, stated in Newsweek 2012, that in his experience, the soul exists separately from the mind and can travel to different dimensions and "this world of consciousness beyond the body, is the true new frontier, not just of science but of humankind itself."

Likewise, the late Dr Wayne Dyer, whom I admire as a spiritual, motivational teacher with his down-to-earth, practical application of the 'law of love' came to me in spirit late one evening, when I was in dire pain after my second hip replacement. Lying down in bed was not comfortable, so I tried to sleep on my sofa and in my discomfort cried out to the Universe to help me overcome the pain. In my prayer, I turned my head to the left to look at a beautiful mirror in the shape of a Church window, where I saw a man's face slowly emerge, gradually floating towards me until his eyes met mine. I immediately recognised Dr Wayne Dyer. I was totally shocked, bewildered and humbled by his presence. He gently spoke to me and I fell into a deep, healing sleep.

When I woke in the morning I couldn't believe the incident and thought perhaps it was a dream but I knew it wasn't! The experience was more real than 'real'. I turned on my computer and staring at me from the screen was a large photo of Wayne. He was smiling as if to verify the encounter and he was offering a free down-load of 'Wishes Fulfilled'. During that morning there were many strange happenings, all related to Wayne and I was compelled to seek communication with him through meditation.

The connection came through easily and we talked about many things, but my real interest was his passageway to the other side - so I asked him about 'death' and his reply was:

"It's impossible to answer that because when you hit the wall it is a different experience for everyone, so you can't say what it's like because everyone's life is unique unto themselves. You hit the wall with what you've got. There's no lying-only truth and most of all love. There is no death!"

We had other conversations, at later dates, but at that time he wanted me to remember, more than anything, that death is only a doorway to another home and that we are 'spirit electric' that can never die and if we choose to live in this amazing construct, our saving grace is to 'love and be loved'.

Death is something we will all face but none of us wish to think about it. The fact that we are all born dying and come willingly to the planet, accepting this premise, doesn't make it any easier for us to admit that none of us will escape our exit. It is interesting to learn that Yair Dor Ziderman's study of the brain claims that it has a mechanism devised to shield us from the thought of death, viewing it as an unfortunate event that happens to other people. This device in the brain which cuts out all thoughts of our own death, helps us to survive and stay alive in dire circumstances, encouraging us to realise it is crucial to live in the present.

New scientific studies undertaken by Professor David Gems at University College London, researching the 'frontiers of ageing' has found that when the process of death ensues, the colour blue radiates from the dying cells in the body and he states that from his evidence 'death is actually a light blue colour', which is very interesting because the colour blue is often used to initiate a feeling of calm, peace and tranquillity and is also employed in hospital operating theatres, swimming pools and other places where antiseptic hygiene is required. It has been found that the colour blue slows down the human metabolism and calms the autonomic system. It is also used to denote technical excellence and is the symbol for attaining a high standard of distinction e.g. being given a blue-ribbon award. It is also said to help to reduce high blood pressure. Additionally it helps the healing process after a surgical operation.

I remember it from my 'electric blue ordeal' when I was visited by Aliens, who utilised an electric blue beam which pulsed and hypnotised me as they performed a minor surgery on a vein in my ankle, where they lodged an implant. I know they have done this to many people and my experience is shared by many. These implants hamper me when I travel, for I am never able to walk through an airport without being stopped and my body x-rayed. The last time I was investigated at an airport, an official said I had seven metal pieces in my body. I was shocked, but somehow I knew they were there, because of my encounters with Alien Greys.

As a small child I could recognise the smell of death with its sweet, sickly, pungent odour and whenever I smelt that essence,

I knew someone was going to die as the pungency would hang around a person, almost as a warning sign that death was imminent. When I was about four years of age whilst I was staying with my grandmother, I wandered to a house a few doors down and casually walked in. The elderly couple living there were both amused and surprised at my visit as I didn't know them, but somehow I seemed to sense their sadness. They greeted me warmly and I sat down on the sofa next to the lady. They didn't seem to know how to entertain a child and gave me some fizzy lemonade in a dusty old glass and a thick catalogue to look at; but it was too heavy for me to hold and I wasn't interested in gardening equipment! As quickly as I had entered the house, I jumped off the sofa and ran out. They must have been very puzzled by my visit. I think it was the sickly-sweet smell that surrounded them that disturbed me and I was glad to run out into the sunlight and fresh air.

I didn't think about the old couple again until the next morning when I went out to play. I heard men speaking seriously, their voices coming from the old people's house. I ran towards it to find men in black suits standing in the yard and from a distance I listened to their conversation about discovering the couple with their heads in the gas oven. They had died together, holding hands. I remembered the smell which still lingered in the air and casually accepted their fate.

In attempting to classify which organ in the body is responsible when we die, for defining who we are, some people identify the brain, the mind, or the heart as containing our real essence, but those organs are only tools to navigate our existence on planet earth. Gregg Braden describes the body as an 'avatar' which contains the soul and as he postulates, the most important ingredient which fuels the container is 'love'.

John Lennon's simple message states, 'all you need is love'...'love is all you need' and many other wonderful songs inspire us to believe that 'love lifts us up where we belong...'

In 'Lucky 2 Love' Lucky speaks from beyond, after her death and through her notes and dictation left for Rosie to decipher, she communicates her message of love and hope, recalling paranormal and psychic experiences which demonstrate beyond doubt that 'there is no death'. For 'love is love and will not fade away!'

THERE IS NO TIME BEYOND TIME

My Dearest Rosie,

If you are reading this letter, then I will have passed on and you will have found the gift I left for you, with the filed notes and instructions for the second Lucky book, containing all the incredible evidence and unbelievable material I have resourced over the years. I know you will do the work justice. I am sorry to leave as we have had some wonderful adventures together, but it's time to go as my mission on earth is complete and further work awaits me beyond. I will not be very far away when you need help. Sometimes you will feel my presence guiding you, so trust in your inner voice and close your eyes to ride with the moment in peaceful meditation and you will be lead in the right direction. Let your higher self-dictate the way forward.

Each time you sit down to piece together the book, ask for Divine inspiration and it will be given. The information I have left you is derived from my meditations, my visions, my bizarre meetings with strange Aliens, my travels into the future and of course my voices. I know you will understand how to present the data to the readers, even though the content is unbelievable to most.

Rosie, my dear, enjoy piecing together this new work for it will bring comfort to those seeking answers and hope to the hopeful and the doubting, bearing in mind that I have only glimpsed the unknown through a tiny crack in the Universe! I will not say 'goodbye', because you have me in all these documents and in your heart and you are in mine...

Rosie folds the letter to her chest while tears flow in the silent room full of magical memories. Everywhere she turns, every photograph, the empty bed, Freddie's old toys and basket reminds her that they are gone and she is determined they will live on through her work.

"Ah there you are Rosie," smiles Estrella peeping from behind the door, "I hope you have found everything?"

Rosie quickly wipes away her tears and meekly returns the smile, adding, "Yes, thank you. She has made everything quite clear and I understand her instructions. I will do my very best to…" her words fade as she breaks down, unable to prevent the floodgate of emotion breaking through her reserved composure.

"Oh don't get upset, she wouldn't want you to cry. She loved you so much Rosie and entrusts you with the next work. She needs you to be strong and decisive in bringing all her material to life. By the way, do you want to work here in her room? We can turn it into an office for you, or would you prefer to work from home?"

The question hadn't occurred to Rosie and for a moment, she is stumped.

"Look think about it and let me know." Estrella smiles reassuringly. "Don't forget you are a member of our family and always welcome. The Sanctuary is her legacy and her life's work continues through us and you are very much a part of everything here, so take your time Rosie, there's no rush."

Estrella leaves Rosie perched on the bed surrounded by files and documents, efficiently numbered and labelled. Absent-mindedly, she picks up a pink file marked 'Beginnings' and reads:

"Hi Rosie- right now you are feeling overwhelmed and don't know where to begin but remember all endings are beginnings and all beginnings are endings, of some sort. When you are lost and have no idea where or how to begin- start with a notion: explore a thought: write it down: expand it: delete it: play around with the concept and take it to its base ending then elevate it to its highest ideal. Most of all don't be afraid of a blank canvass. Good Luck!"

Rosie sighs with conviction as though she has suddenly made an important decision and says out loud to herself..."yes! I'll work here!" and begins to sort the folders in numerical order on the dressing table, leaving the first file on the bed to peruse. Without thinking she lies down in her mistress's place and opens the manuscript and begins to read:

MY DEATH VISION

My death is joyous.

It is Christmas Eve and my grandsons and I gaze up at the night sky catching a glimmer of a shooting star exploding across the galaxy, but it is not a star, it is a ship from my planet. My people are coming to take me home. We watch as the silver disc slowly descends and comes to rest a few feet off the frosty lawn. My boys tenderly hold my hands, sensing my departure, as I rise out of my body and dance across the grass with Freddie bouncing and jumping at my heels. My grandsons observe two luminescent beings lift Freddie and I into the craft and for a few moments the silver shell of the ship shimmers and glows in the dark, then disappears into the night. As I leave they feel my kiss like a breath of warm air on their cheeks and they know I will always love them. Echoing from afar in the cold night air, I hear their voices exclaiming softly to their mother and younger sister - "Nanny has gone home!"

As I step inside the craft, the outer casing of the ship shrinks like a thin micro-film of stretched bubble gum. I sit in a little solo seat with Freddie on my knee and at first it is as though I am floating above the ground in an invisible bubble. I feel the outside, inside as we glide across the fields. The movement of the craft is unlike anything I have ever experienced. Floating noiselessly above the ground, I am part of the earth and the pulse of the planet pounds within me together with all living beings. As we zoom into the void the speed increases, racing faster than the speed of light and then everything disappears in a flash through a black portal, into another universe.

"Oh I'm sorry Rosie, I didn't know you were still here," Estrella interrupts.

"I have decided to stay here and work, if it's ok with you?"

"Of course! I'll make sure you have everything you need! I think she will be happy that you are here!"

The two women smile and a ray of sunlight falls on Freddie's empty basket.

"Well I must get on. See you later Rosie, oh and by the way I'll have a desk and some office equipment sent up." Estrella breezes out leaving Rosie to resume reading the notes.

Rosie, 'Imagine a time when time is no more and has no meaning, for it is a man-made earth structure which turns living into a race to avoid death. When we are in our earth mode we are encapsulated in a devised diurnal rhythm of - morning/noon/night...morning/noon/night - imprisoning us in a compound cycle from the moment we are born. On entering the planet with its inbuilt urgency of beating the clock, like grains of sand sifting through an egg-timer, we spend the rest of our lives competing against the time bomb ticking inside our minds and bodies. We don't want to grow old and die. We want to be forever young, but we are born dying and have to accept our fate and once freed from earth's time zone, time has no meaning. I know, I have felt it, for I have travelled beyond earth's electric fence, floated in nothingness and experienced the endlessness of time without time, free from a beginning or ending - but it is not a void. I glimpsed this state briefly when I was given a meditation by my whisperers, based on the colour, 'black' and as you know Rosie, I was shown a new meditation system based on 'Colour Vibration' and you helped to document the material for my book 'The Gates of Eden'. If you recall, I told you that the colour black is not a negative vibration. It was created to give us peace and rest and the chance to retreat from overpowering influences that taunt us during the day. Night was shaped in blackness and silver moonlight crafted to help human consciousness fly back to its origin, through sleep. I am sharing this with you as I want you to have an understanding of the formlessness and timelessness of what lies beyond, when the body is discarded. I want to share a little of my 'state of being' with you because you will wonder what has happened to me and although I cannot vouch for sure that it will be so, I just know I have had visions of the condition of 'timelessness'. The meditation I was given on the colour 'black' is very useful and you might want to use it when you need to escape the world, you can record it to pass on to help others.

As you know, my system of meditation differs from other techniques, in that other methods require you to still your mind and clear your monkey brain of continual chatter. Most people find this very difficult, but with my method instead of removing all thoughts from your mind, you fill it with a journey and in following the journey, you trick the mind into falling into a state of deep receptivity to healing and higher self-awareness. Every colour on earth has a purpose and a unique electric vibration exuding light which affects all living cells. Colour is conscious energy and humans are conscious beings, so the interaction of the two together can be very powerful, especially when directed towards healing. When we choose to seek the power of colour energy and harness the strength to help us tune into a higher realm, the result can be astounding. The method to use when going into a meditative state is to read the journey a few times so that your mind will memorise details or record the journey and then play it back as you enter a meditative state. Use my breathing technique - 'the breath of the sea' which is to breathe in for four counts and slowly exhale for four counts. Do this three times and you will enter an altered state to follow the journey in your mind. Close your eyes and take the journey:

COLOUR 'BLACK' MEDITATION JOURNEY TO UNDERSTAND 'TIMELESSNESS' FOR INNER PEACE

"It's a grey winter's day, cold, damp and still. You are walking alone through a quiet town and are drawn towards the bright lights of a large store. As you enter, through the automatic doors, the heat warms your face and the smell of damp air from outside lingers for a few moments. There is hardly anyone around, only a few assistants checking stock lists and gossiping quietly. The warmth makes you drowsy and you decide to have a rest in the restaurant on the second floor. You wait while the shiny silver lift pings a welcome, as the door opens. You step inside the steel box and press the red button to the second floor. You feel the motion glide upwards and upwards and as you float on and on, you are peaceful and calm. Gently the lift halts and the door silently slides open. Blackness, heavy like soft velvet waits to embrace you and emptiness like the deep, dark void of space hovers to caress you. The motionless blackness is heavy with a still, soft breath drawing you forward into the nothingness. You step out blindly. There is no fear of falling for your feet are light and you float onwards to luminescent beings who wait to greet you. There is no fear. Blackness is soft and comforting. Blackness is all- encompassing, womblike, safe and protective, engulfing you in a mantle of loving care, so strong that you forget the pressure of living and surrender to the moment of timeless drifting. The hands of loving beings guide you to rest where all life's burdens disintegrate and fade into oblivion. Anxiety, strain, tension- all are soothed as you give yourself permission to be at peace and allow the experience of nothingness, realising nothing really matters because in the 'elsewhere' beyond the beyond there is no time: no urgency: no emergency: no limits: no decisions, there is only you. In the 'no time' zone you remain until every cell of your being is renewed. When you are restored spiritually and physically, you rise without effort and float back through the blackness towards a small tunnel of light growing larger as you approach and within a moment's breath you are back standing inside the lift descending to the ground floor. The door opens swiftly and you are back in the bright, busy store. You glance at the clock and note that only a few minutes have passed since you first entered the lift, but timewise in your mind you have travelled far. Earth time has accounted for little but cosmic time is limitless and as you walk into the cold afternoon where a weak, watery sun breaks through a dark scudding cloud, you have no fear, for you have known the timeless zone and have the knowledge to travel there whenever you seek peace."

Rosie sighs and pauses, sensing her mistress close by. "I know you are here," she whispers in the unreal silence, "please just show me a sign, I don't disbelieve but...please just...?"

A gentle gust of wind sails through an open window and rustles the notes lying on the dressing table. Selectively, a shabby piece of paper flutters to the floor and Rosie carefully picks it up and reads:

"Think Lucky and you will be Lucky. Shape and alter your mind-set to be positive at all times and only good energy will steer your thoughts. Be your thoughts in action."

Rosie clutches the note to her chest and thanks the Universe for showing her a sign. Now she is ready to go home after a wondrous day, happy to bear the responsibility of chronicling Lucky 2 Love and content to have the support and strength from her mistress, guiding her from beyond, who is and forever will be her 'Lucky'.

⊷⊶◅◇▻⊷⊶

THINK LUCKY AND YOU WILL BE LUCKY

Well Rosie,

Today I am sitting peacefully in the conservatory watching the birds preening their feathers and splashing in the little bird bath Augustus made for them. He keeps the garden beautiful in all seasons and I am so grateful to him for his dedication to the Sanctuary. Everyone who comes here always admires his handy work. On this glorious spring morning I am going back in search of Lucky, remembering her words to steer me through all difficulties: "Think Lucky and you will be Lucky".

Breathing deeply, I allow myself to go under, into a swirling mist and to travel swiftly towards a circle of light, arriving in dazzling sunshine and standing on the side of a mountain nestled close to a range of peaks. It reminds me of my mountaineering days in Wales when I was a teenager. Inhaling the fresh, invigorating air, my lungs expand and I feel whole again. I am dressed appropriately for mountain walking, complete with tough brown boots, thick woollen socks and a long dark-green waxed coat. I am leaning on a tall wooden staff with a beautifully crafted goat's head handle, carved in polished bone. Staring at the magnificent range of mountains surrounding me, I am humbled in the presence of nature's giants, who like sleeping gods, wait for the call to rise. The grasses quiver and the wind sighs across the valley where little spring buds gather in clusters over the meadows and tips of yellow and purple blossom peep through the mossy-green cracks in the rocks. It is like the time before the darkness enveloped the planet and atomic radiation burnt the earth to a dry desert cinder.

I am here in the now of another scene, in another mode and I wonder what awaits me. I know Lucky has new assignments, new adventures, new challenges ahead and the distant past seems like another lifetime in another body, when Lucky was searching for her daughter. The serum that was injected into her by Seth, the reptilian, which made her regress back into her youth, lasted a short while before she returned to her timeline to be reunited with her daughter and it was as though their years apart simply melted away. Together they set up a healing centre -'The Sanctuary' and helped many people. Now, in the light of that goodness, Lucky is free to enter different states of awareness to record information from both past and future to help people raise their higher consciousness onto a greater vibration. Knowledge of what has been and what is to come helps when making important decisions. It is said that 'the future's not ours to see' but if someone has a glimpse of what might be, to enlighten others, then in the light of that knowledge, everyone has a chance to make an informed choice for the future.

Now in the consciousness of Lucky, I stare beyond the sun-glazed peaks to where the bright sky meets the earth, aware that I am alone again. Not lonely, but in the state of 'aloneness' which keeps my mind alert and tuned in to outside forces and although I miss my family, I know I must face these challenges alone. I scan the mountain path and my heart leaps, as racing towards me is a fluffy bundle of mischief.

"Oh Freddie! Have they allowed you to come back to me? Oh my darling doggy!" I croon as I pick him up and cuddle him. His soft curly fur brushes my face as he snuggles into my shoulder. I am not sure which direction to take but Freddie knows and bounds up the grassy gradient wagging his blonde, curly-fronded tail, that flutters like tiny Tibetan prayer flags in the wind. I follow him up a gravel path until we reach a stone-built, grey-slated cottage encompassed by a grey-slate wall that is swathed in bright yellow dandelions and weeds, sprouting from the untended cracks. Freddie sits and waits by the gate panting, his little pink tongue hanging out. He is so proud to lead me to my new destination. "Is this it Freddie?" I call and he barks affirmatively, impatient for me to follow. Cautiously I open the gate but he is already at the porch waiting to be let in.

The ancient cottage door has an old-fashioned wooden handle set in a brass case and squeaks as I push it open. I place my staff in an old china umbrella stand, conveniently set by the front porch and shake off my boots. I smell a coal fire burning and feel the welcoming heat as I enter. An old, brown leather armchair waits by the fireside and Freddie lies down on the faded rag rug next to it. A tiny, dull-green kitchenette sink and cupboards are in the far left of the room, with an old-fashioned aga dominating the back wall. Little floral curtains match the orange cushions and lino and a small door leads to a bedroom where a pink candlewick bedspread is laid neatly across a small wooden bed. A tiny but adequate bathroom with an old bath, sink and toilet is to the right of the sitting room. Everything is compact, neat and clean and I guess the cottage must have belonged to a farmer and his wife who chose to spend a lifetime together in the secluded wilderness. Suddenly, a high-pitched mechanical voice chimes:

"Please take your seat and wait for instruction. Please take your seat and wait for instruction!" I am not sure where the voice is coming from and the only seat is the armchair by the fire, so I quickly obey orders and sit down. The room darkens, operated from an invisible source and everything fades into a blackout. The windows electronically seal and are shuttered. Both front and side doors lock automatically with heavy steel bolts shooting into place as the walls morph into a kaleidoscopic cinema showing star maps and a live newscast from Mars and the Moon. The whole building is transformed into an amazing technological centre. Who would have suspected that a tiny ancient cottage could be fitted with the most incredible modern equipment? Suddenly from a control panel, which now hides the sink, the image of a man appears and quickly comes into focus revealing Colonel J.R. Gerald, an American, in charge of 'operations'. Last time, in my little chalet by the sea in Cornwall, the Colonel was projected through holographic technology to teach and prepare me for the pending assignment and his presence was so real, it was as though he was actually in the room. This time the technology is far superior with greater depth of texture and intense images and the Colonel walks towards me completely realistically, carrying a small chair and sits down opposite me. I feel I can almost reach out and touch him- the only thing that spoils the illusion is that his feet are not visible. "Well, now, it's been a while since we last spoke, many things have happened since then and there are changes across the board. By the way, down in the basement is a fully equipped gym and when you go down there an instructor will appear. You are very unfit for the next assignment and you will be expected to train every day and follow a strict regime. Oh, and I nearly forgot to say that the whole of the cottage is sound-proofed, so be careful not to lock yourself in, as no one will hear you, even if you scream."

I wasn't too sure if I liked that idea but nodded just to please him.

"You know you can opt out of all of this at any time. You don't have to carry out the assignment, I mean if you would sooner return to your people and forget the earth plan or choose to reincarnate and experience a different life-it's up to you- the choices are yours."

I listen to his words but my sense of duty urges me to agree to undertake the assignment.

"Ok, ok, that's fine then, you will begin your schedule in the morning. Remember what I said about acting from your Primary and Secondary source when you were undergoing training in Cornwall?" I nod and he pauses, checking my reaction before continuing.

"In this next assignment, you will be required at all times to act from your Primary source - that is you have to put yourself first at all times. If you are killed it's no good to any of us. Remember a soldier always defends himself first, so you *must* be fit for purpose!"

"She could always be re-generated in one of our new centres!" says a woman wearing a white coat who has crept in behind the Colonel, her dark hair swept back in a French pleat. She looks very officious.

"This is Dr Zoburg," the Colonel says." She will be responsible for preparing your health programme for the mission."

I smile to acknowledge her but she doesn't respond. Her unfriendly attitude makes me wonder what the mission entails, as it seems there is great emphasis on getting fit for the operation and from her manner I glean she doesn't think I'm up to it!

"You see soldier- one thing's for sure, it's the number one priority that you are fighting fit, otherwise we won't send you. Your heart and body have to be strong."

"With our training, Colonel, she will be! She will undergo a tight physical regime together with a controlled diet." She fixes me with a steely gaze. "In the fridge you have day one calorie counted meal. You will eat no more, no less than what is prepared for you. Understood?"

I nod and mumble, "Yes, yes of course!"

"Well I guess that's it for now? Good to see you soldier. I'll be in touch!" The Colonel's image flickers and both he and the doctor disappear. The cottage, with its amazing technology resumes its quaint camouflage as the techno-equipment slides away into the walls, the bolts on the doors glide back into hidden cavities and the bars and shutters at the windows disappear. Not one single techno detail is left and the little place once again smiles innocently on the world outside.

In the strange quiet of the moment Freddie jumps on my knee and licks my hand. He must be hungry and thirsty so I carry him to the kitchen and look for dog food. I am disappointed that they have forgotten Freddie's needs but inside a drawer I find a note explaining that Freddie is a cyber dog, an exact replica of the original Freddie in every way, except that he doesn't need feeding or to be given water. I am shocked. He seems so real and his perky personality is the same as before. The note reads:

'Do not give your cyber-pet water or any other liquid as it will destroy his inner mechanism. Do not feed him organic matter of any kind. We thought you would enjoy his company. You have much to learn and achieve in a short space of time, which will be easier for you to manage if your pet is virtual."

How can Freddie not be real? He is so life-like with his little beating heart, his shiny, expressive eyes and his warm little pink tongue. I hold his head close to my face and whisper:

"Who cares if you are not real Freddie? I love you all the same and I suppose I don't have to worry about feeding you or taking you out at night." I place him down and watch him scamper around chasing his tail just like the old Freddie and I am happy he is with me even if he is just a hi-tech toy!

Outside the light is dimming and I close the pretty floral curtains to feel cosy. I suddenly remember the coal fire and look for the coal bucket to stack it up, but there isn't one. I spy the note on the mantelpiece which reads:

'Don't worry about the coal fire, it is illusory and will self- adjust to your command. If it is cold just ask for more heat and if it is too warm just state 'cool down'. It will continue to heat the house and water as long as you command it to do so.'

I am surprised as the coal fire looks so authentic and sends out real heat, but like Freddie, it is virtual. I wonder what else isn't real and look in the fridge. Neatly stacked are two containers marked 'day one'. I take them out of the fridge and open them. The food looks good and nutritious with pasta, seafood and vegetables with a note on the top container with instructions:

'Do not use the aga for cooking as it is purely for show. The fridge is a fridge-freezer and a cooker. The uncooked containers have an in-built cooking programme. Place them in the top drawer to start the cooking process. When the cooking time is complete a green light will appear at the top of the fridge. Remove the containers from the drawer. Enjoy your meals.'

Once more I am amazed at the high-technology of everything. I want a drink. I need alcohol to soothe my nerves and to cope with the unreal reality of the situation. I search everywhere for anything... wine, whiskey, liqueurs...but there is nothing except a curt note in the drinks cabinet that says-

"You are not allowed alcohol. It is strictly forbidden for your training!"

"DAMN!" I curse. I begin to doubt my commitment to the whole set-up. I slump down on my only chair feeling depressed and defeated. Freddie jumps up on my knee and cuddles in close. I snuggle into his warm fur for comfort, musing about my choices. The Colonel said that

I don't have to do the assignment but I battle with myself, craving to be relieved from the difficult path ahead and yet curious about the mission. I ask my whisperers for guidance and close my eyes in readiness to connect with them. Gently from a deep well within, a voice becomes clear and speaks softly;

"Remember a time when all seemed bleak? You had just given birth to your fourth child and she screamed most of the time, almost driving you insane. Remember that Monday morning when chaos reigned? Your eldest daughter needed money for her cookery lesson; your second daughter had lost her P.E. kit, which you eventually tracked down in the wash basket; your little son was crying because someone had broken his favourite yellow toy truck and the baby was howling and you, in your distress, sprayed your hair with deodorant and squirted hair spray under your arm pits. The baby messed in the bath and you counted out your last spare change for dinner money for your daughters. It was snowing heavily and you had to walk your son to his nursery school manoeuvring the pram through the slush. It was especially hard as, suffering with mastitis, you had a high fever and you suspected that your husband was having an affair. Everything seemed stacked against you as you trudged through the mud and sludge down a small street where delivery vans splashed you and the pram.

You had no money left in your purse to buy groceries and arrived too early at the post office to collect the family allowance. The bright lights of Mothercare enticed you inside the large store, where you took shelter for a while. Near the door was a 'sale' rail and you sifted through a few items before spying the most beautiful, knitted, pink baby coat with cerise fur embroidered around the hood, tied with lovely little pink ribbons. It had been reduced to £5.50. You stood staring at it for ages, imagining your baby girl wearing it, but you were miserable because you had no money to buy it. Just as you were wishing you had the money, you felt a gush of cold air whip open the door and you thought someone was standing behind you, but when you looked, there was no one there. It was time to go to the post office, and as you turned the pram around an old lady stopped you and handed you a pound coin explaining that she had seen you drop it. You denied it, but she insisted that you took it. You placed it carefully in your pocket and arriving at the post office, just as you tilted the pram upwards to mount the entrance step, something clinked off the wheel and to your surprise another pound coin lay on the floor. You put it inside your pocket and continued towards the queue where a man stopped you and handed you a pound coin saying that you had dropped it from your coat pocket. This time you were shocked but politely accepted the money. Suddenly, you had three pounds that had appeared from nowhere. Further into the queue another pound coin appeared by your foot and you asked around to see if anyone had dropped it, but no one had. Just as you rounded the corner to go to the desk another pound appeared by the pram wheel. You had five pounds! At the desk the woman gave you the right amount of family allowance and when you opened your purse to put in the loose change you went white and dizzy. The lady at the counter thought you were going to faint and offered you a glass of water, but you recovered your composure realising that there was now fifty pence in your purse, where previously you had nothing. So from nowhere you had £5.50 to buy the treasured little coat for your baby. You never knew where the money came from and as you left Mothercare with the little coat, you thanked the universe for giving you an amazing miracle and vowed never to forget it. You see, miracles can and do happen and being reminded of that bleak time when your voice in the wilderness was heard, remember the joy of that moment and apply it to your situation. Remember you are never lost, you are never alone because help is closer to you than the air you breathe."

The voice fades and I smile remembering the miracle. I am grateful for the help I received and realise that it's not the alcohol I need to provide calming reassurance, but the answer to melting away all my fears lies inside myself. I have the strength to face what awaits me and with renewed confidence I walk over to the fridge/cooker to prepare my first meal. I follow the instructions and within ten seconds the food is ready. It tastes surprisingly good and the meal is very filling. I saunter over to the sink to get water to find another note is balancing on top of the tap that reads:

'Do not use the water. The tap water is not safe to drink. Water is supplied at the side of the fridge where you will find cold water, hot water, ice, hot tea, cold tea, hot coffee, cold coffee, cold milk, hot milk and a selection of herbal teas. ENJOY'

Once more I am amazed at the technological wizardry and try out the cold-water button. An image of a bamboo cup filled with cold water appears on a screen and then it manifests itself on a plastic shelf. The water tastes like fresh spring water from the mountain and I marvel at the ease of tele- transportation of material matter, conjured from nowhere. I remember when teleportation was a concept in Sci-fi films and not reality, but alien knowledge and co-operation with humans sped up the world's thirst for technological advancement and helped to equip planet earth with cosmic innovation. I am plunged into techno-genius without any preparation or training and I know I have to adapt quickly to the new state of living or I will fail miserably at the mission. Learning that things around me are illusory and realizing Freddie is a cyborg and that nothing of any significance is real; I feel like Alice in Wonderland, falling down the rabbit hole. Now I am tired and search for the light switch. I am not surprised to find a note on the wall with light control instructions which states simply:

'To turn the lights on say' lights on' and to turn them off say 'lights off'. I laugh to myself wondering what kind of voice to use, I test out a few and discover that the equipment responds to any voice simply reacting to key words. I lie down on the quaint little bed which is comfortable and especially cosy and as Freddie curls up beside me, I wonder if cyber dogs sleep. The cyber-pet manual I found in a drawer said that the pet automatically adjusts to its owner's routine and at bedtime it switches itself off and wakes when the owner's breathing changes. It's not like having a real dog and more like going to bed with a sophisticated toy, but I suppose he is a cute substitute for my real Freddie. My command for 'lights out' is immediately obeyed and I am conscious of hearing my own voice echo loudly in the silence. Freddie is motionless and I guess he has switched himself off - I wish sleep was that easy for me. I am nervous and uncertain of what the morning may bring but I am optimistic that I will be lucky and pass my fitness tests after training because I know that if I think lucky, I will be lucky for I am LUCKY.

⊰•❈•⊱

TECHNO-MANIA

Freddie barks and jumps up on my chest, just like he did in the old days when he always knew the moment I was awake - I guess my breathing pattern changed, alerting his cyber mechanism to take action. "Wachet Auf! Wachet Auf!" A voice commands sternly and I jump out of bed with Freddie chasing after me. In the kitchen my breakfast is prepared and a note gives the time of our first fitness session. I have half an hour to eat and get ready. It is odd not taking Freddie for his early morning walk and even stranger not giving him food. I am nervous and not hungry to eat the muesli, so I push away the bowl but a bell rings and a voice demands that I finish it. I pull it back immediately and the ringing ceases. I force down the food and head for the bathroom. I have ten minutes to dress and tie back my hair before the session begins. "Where the hell is the basement? I say out loud. I scurry up and down the little cottage but can't find the entrance to the gym and time is racing. I mustn't be late. Frustrated, I shout out;

"Ok! Ok! If I am to train, show me where the blasted entrance is?"

Suddenly a loud whooshing sound, like a hurricane, sweeps through the kitchen and a steel door appears at the side of the bedroom. It slides open as I step towards it and I run down a flight of steps into a massive gymnasium. A Chinese instructor appears and bows and says;

"My name is Lee Wan Chu. I am your trainer for fitness."

I bow awkwardly, returning his gesture as Dr Zoburg emerges from behind a large weighing machine and asks me to sit in the harness. She records my weight, my blood pressure and my heartrate.

"Mmm," she exclaims, clearly unimpressed," this is not good! Do your best Lee Wan. Good luck!" With that she disappears leaving Lee Wan observing me with a sour expression. I take a deep breath and follow him to a running machine. It looks just like the traditional ones but the moment I step on it, I am transported to the bottom of a very steep hill and hear the command 'run!'. I try really hard at first, but the going is tough and my asthma prevents me from breathing properly. I don't have the stamina to keep going. I stop and look up at the hill. Cold sweat trickles down my back. I can't go on! 'Run!' commands the voice but I stay bent over trying to catch my breath. A sharp electric pain pierces my head. 'RUN! RUN!' commands the voice. I begin to cry and through my tears, pick up my feet and attempt to run. My heart hurts. My head aches. My legs are heavy and my feet are sore. Another sharp electric shock pierces my chest and a voice shouts: 'RUN! RUN!' I force my body to straighten up and vaguely lift my feet. I tell myself to run but somehow I just can't! The shock tactics continue and I drag my body forwards until I finally reach the top of the hill only to find another waiting in the distance. "I can't! I can't!" I plead, panting to gain my breath, but the invisible voice attacks until I lift my feet but now, my legs crumble and I black out.

"There, what did I tell you?" I hear Dr Zoburg exclaim triumphantly. "I told you she'd never make it!"

I open my eyes and look up at the ceiling from my collapsed position on the floor.

"Try again!" Lee Wan says authoritatively. "Get up! Try again!"

I struggle to sit up but my head spins and I flop back.

"We have to report this to the Colonel and see what he thinks about the situation. In the meantime get her out of here!" commands the Doctor.

I wake up in the small bed with the pink candlewick bedspread neatly tucked in at the corners like a hospital bed. As I open my eyes I see someone standing close, dressed in white holding a tray.

"Greetings Madam. I am Serdonis. I have been sent to look after you. Please sit up and take your medicine."

Serdonis steps forward and lowers the tray towards me. He looks like a human but I know he is an android which doesn't surprise me, as most things in the cottage are not what they seem.

"What medicine is it and what's it for?" I ask, uneasily.

"Well Madam it is not for you to question, although it is a reasonable question, so I will endeavour to answer it. I will inject into your vein an energy cell which will whiz around your body to regenerate all dying cells. If you were adept at self- healing you could apply this process yourself, but I see you are not."

I open my mouth to answer but he turns towards me saying: "look I will show you how it is done." His chest slides open to reveal a screen on which an educational video plays. It shows a woman breathing deeply, her eyes closed in meditation. From the top of her head she sends a bright, white light of energy down into her body where all her major organs light up as the energy passes through her body.

"You see" Serdonis says, "this deep healing meditation system restores the whole body but you have to be a Master healer to achieve this. Imagine your body as a house and as you move through it, you switch on all the lights as you pass the major organs, generating light to each part of the house and the light engenders a healing warmth throughout your body. Conversely, of course, this method can be used on an enemy whereby you enter the victim's body through meditation and can slash at his heart with a virtual knife- causing a great deal of harm, probably killing him!"

"Really?" I question.

"Oh yes, it is very effective. When you imagine entering a person's body, you can project light to inflict pain. For example you can project the energy beam to the heart and cause a heart attack!"

"Oh my goodness!" I gasp. "I had no idea that could happen."

"It's a weapon that's been in use for a very long time - very much like in Voodoo, black magic. Similarly, our agents, who are highly trained, can glean information secretly stored in a person's mind. It's easiest during sexual activity. The agent lures the subject into sexual arousal and during the act of sex, when the energy reaches peak level, the agent is able to enter the subject's mind, which during the heightened sensation of orgasm, expands and opens to reveal all secrets, thus the agent can steal any amount of information. It's called Sexpionage!"

"Wow!" I exclaim. My innocence and curiosity spur him on to reveal more.

"Oh yes, we have many devices to unlock secrets stored in the mind. For example 'skin receptors'.

"Skin receptors?" I ask.

"Yes 'skin receptors' are like invisible plastic suckers which stick to your finger-tips, are attached to nerve endings and are devised to pick up electrical pulses from the subject, which are then transmitted to the receiver. Skin receptors are also used to replace your own fingerprints with someone else's. Today they're mostly used to gain access into secret places by using another person's finger-print code."

"That's incredible!" I exclaim as Serdonis continues, eager to inform and enlighten me.

"Yes, you see 'skin receptors' with their powerful frequencies can also build up emotional states in a victim to such a height that the controller can manipulate a person to commit heinous crimes and murder masses of people."

"Ohh!" I exclaim, which provokes Serdonis to continue, his manner excited and agitated.

"Yes you see, the mind is an incredible computer and can be used to store secret information. Our agents can use other peoples' minds to store secret information in compartments, with the owner having absolutely no idea they exist. The agent uses a small device, like a pocket pen, which when pointed at the host can freeze them physically and mentally, during which time the agent implants the information in the secret pocket of the host's mind."

"You mean a little like the 'Men In Black' films where the agents freeze the victim and deletes their memory?" I ask.

"Well, it's a little more sophisticated than that, but you've got the picture." Serdonis nods.

"But what happens when the agent wants to retrieve the secret information?"

"Good question! Deserves a good answer. The agent uses the device again to freeze the victim, retrogrades the process and seals the secret compartment. The victim never knows they have been used."

"Serdonis - that is enough! The patient does not want to be bothered by unnecessary data. Has the injection been administered?" demands Dr Zoburg.

"Not yet Doctor, I am just about to complete the task," replies Serdonis, winking, as I allow him to inject me. Almost immediately I experience a warmth spreading throughout my body, like lying in balmy sunshine. I am left in peace to sleep but when I wake a team of experts, discussing my health stand around the bed. With my eyes still closed, I listen to their conversation.

"Well, it's impossible to regenerate her heart, I mean it's worn out!"

"Yes, she has been around for a long time. Longer than most I suppose!"

"We could re-birth her and bring her back to her early twenties."

"That's a possibility, but she would have to forfeit all her memories of her previous earth life."

"Look, to perform the assignment she has to be in tip-top condition, otherwise the teleport will kill her!"

"Or the radiation!"

Cold fear seeps into my consciousness and I inadvertently twitch, alerting the team to the fact that that I am awake.

"That's it... take it easy... sit up slowly. You'll feel a little nauseous, but that will soon pass," adds a nurse.

I obey and sit up to look at the health team who are holding little silver gadgets like ball point pens which, when aimed at me directly, record the state of my health, the condition of my heart, liver and lungs and monitors the effectiveness of my inner organs.

"How are you feeling?" enquires Dr Zoborg.

"I'm fine, but I'd be a lot better if you explained what all this is about!" I retort.

For a moment there is an awkward silence followed by an exchange of glances and then Dr Zoborg gathers up her team and promptly exits, leaving me to stare at Freddie's basket where he lies motionless. I guess they have turned him off. It occurs to me to use a verbal command to wake him, seeing as most things in the cottage are voice controlled, so I call out, 'Freddie wake up!" and instantaneously he sits up panting, his little pink tongue hanging out. I pat the bed and he jumps up to be cuddled. My mind wanders years and years back, to a toy called a Tamagotchie. It was a tiny cyber-pet where young children would take care of a computer animal following orders to feed it, take it for walks, give it sleep periods and play times, all of which were virtual activities. If the Tamagotchie pet didn't receive enough attention it died and turned itself off. The toy became all the rage at the time, every child wanted one and it became an obsessive occupation with many children. I could see that, at the time the toy was an introduction to future cyber-pets and also a way to tie youngsters to virtual reality, instead of them experiencing the real world. Luckily parents gradually found substitute toys for their children, steering them away from the computer attachment.

Another toy which alarmed me around the same time was an alien egg which, when kept in the fridge overnight turned into a baby alien made of a gooey, gelatinous, sticky, slimy substance that came in many different colours. I thought it was a way to introduce the idea of extra-terrestrials to children so they wouldn't be afraid when aliens were finally declared 'real' beings. Unfortunately, for fifteen-year-old delinquent boys it was an ideal substance to throw around the classroom as it stuck to the walls and anything it touched. At the time

I was teaching music to un-cooperative teenagers, who, during one lesson decided to go to war using the baby aliens as ammunition to fire at each other. I was attacked by one of the boys as I tried to break up the fracas and had to be rescued by the deputy head. I was really glad when the alien baby slime craze died out.

"Can you walk? A young nurse enquires as she pops her head around the door. I nod and tentatively get out of bed to follow her into the sitting room where the team are assembled with a holographic Colonel, minus his legs, is seated on a stool.

"Ah there you are soldier... come in... come in... sit down," welcomes the Colonel.

I nervously sit in the armchair while the health team in their white coats take notes on minute computers that are the size of small matchboxes.

"Well, I expect you are wondering what this is all about and why all the medical fuss etcetera?" the Colonel asks, while he shuffles a load of papers on his knee, keeping his eyes fixed on my face.

"To be frank, it's a little complicated and you will have to take a leap of faith and trust us to guide you through this assignment. You have failed your physical test on every count and that is disastrous and detrimental to the requirements of the mission. However, mentally, psychically, intellectually and emotionally you tick all the boxes. So the team and I have decided to offer you the chance to 'rebirth' reincarnating you at the age of twenty five years. Unfortunately, however, the process will obliterate all past memories of this lifetime."

He pauses waiting for my response as I try to take in his proposal. In the silence, the white coats exchange glances as I mull over the implications of losing my identity from my present life.

"I'm sorry, but I can't make a decision without knowing the full details of the mission and what exactly the 'rebirthing entails." I say firmly, sensing their eagerness for me to comply with their wishes.

"Ok, ok I understand, it's a perfectly reasonable request, but it will take some time to fully explain everything, so I suggest everyone take a seat," requests the Colonel.

From nowhere five chairs manifest themselves for the team and they sit in a semi-circle around the holographic Colonel. He presses a hand-held remote gadget and the tiny sitting room turns into a techno-equipped conference room complete with 3D screens bouncing off three walls.

"So let's begin!" the Colonel commands. "In the future, around 2090, time travel is commonplace and efficient teleport machines are a reliable mode of travelling backwards, or forwards in time. Unfortunately, the real deal is very expensive and so cheap travel is offered to ordinary citizens on the black market. Mafia dealers trade in secret underground tunnels and provide unstable, uncertain, insecure and unsafe journeys for those willing to pay vast amounts of currency and not necessarily money but other luxuries including trading slaves or the exchange of a son or daughter in return for the coveted one-way trip.

Suddenly the three 3D walls suck us into the future. The year 2090 pops up on the screen and we find ourselves inside an underground illicit 'teleport time machine' station. It is dark, dingy and excruciatingly hot. The air is putrid with the stench of unwashed bodies, seeping sewage tanks and a strange fuel smell that isn't petrol, diesel, white spirit or alcohol but rather a mixture of all those components, which catches in the back of our throats. We shield our mouths with our hands as we follow a long line of people waiting to board the teleport time machine. Each person approaches the boarding gate, quaking and fearfully obeying the rough guards' commands. The Colonel speaks to us through the noisy mayhem:

"As you can see, these people are desperate to go back to the past; the past we inhabit now. They have many reasons for sacrificing everything to return. They miss our clean air, the freedom of family life, decent, non-chemical food or they have curative remedies from the future they want to take back to heal a family member or friend. Some go back with lottery winning details and win vast amounts of money through their prior knowledge and millions are also won with information on horse and greyhound racing and other forms of betting. Criminals from the future want to escape into the past where they will be untraceable. Others want to return to the past to the time zone when space travel is on the verge of becoming a reality so that they can be part of the first colony to be sent to Mars. But most disconcerting of all is that, in our 'now' we are being attacked from the future by terrorists who want to change the present, striving for world domination with weapons from the future which can annihilate our planet. But I digress. As you can see, there are so many frantic people anxious to escape the future who are willing to pay almost anything to return to the past.

"So are these illicit time travel machines dangerous?" I ask.

"Indeed they are!" replies the Colonel, sighing, "indeed they are, you see unless the machines are government designed and approved, they are death traps. Many people are torn apart and their bodies burnt from the inside out through radiation leaks from the machines. Some arrive naked in the wrong places and are immediately hunted down and shot by the inter-teleport frontier guards who recognise the travellers from the numbers branded on their wrists."

"Branded? That's so brutal and primitive!" I retort.

"Indeed it is!" Adds the Colonel sympathetically," but it's the only sure way that the number stays on the skin, as other methods are not as reliable and tend to fade in the electrical process. Now, watch and learn."

We are sucked into a disturbing scene as the 3D screens envelope us into the murky illicit travel procedure and we witness the awful process. We see an old woman stripped naked and branded on her wrist with a small gadget like an old-fashioned hair curling tong. She flinches and grits her teeth through the pain. She walks onto a rickety wooden platform carrying a small case, every traveller is allowed to take one case or bag for important documents, basic clothes and another item of their choice. She waits in the middle of a painted white square on the boards and a wire cage descends over her. As the cage drops, it bursts into purple electrical flames with sparks and lightning bolts streaking into the crowd. (I am reminded of the piece of equipment designed by Nikola Tesla, who it is said, received information from an Alien race on how to build extraordinary technologically advanced, futuristic machinery. Some believe he built a time machine which the American government secretly acquired).

We watch, horrified as the process fails and the poor woman is burnt alive from the inside, leaving her skeleton dangling from one of the wire bars, with flaps of unburnt skin hanging precariously like raw meat in a butcher's shop. It is a disgusting and disturbing sight for everyone to witness like a public hanging and cleaners quickly hop inside the cage to clear up the bones and scrape off the bits of skin left sizzling on the bars. The smell of roasting flesh sears the air like a cannibalistic barbeque. The crowd recoil in revulsion but the manager urges them back in line saying the old woman hadn't followed the instructions of fasting before the trip and that was why she was burnt by radiation.

Next in line is a naked young man who nervously approaches the boarding gate, shaking with fear. Urine trickles down his legs and the cleaners are ordered to wipe him dry before the cage descends. He clutches his little brown case to his genitals and closes his eyes tightly as the purple electric force engulfs him and he disappears into the ether. Everyone gasps and sighs, clapping gleefully in relief, assured that the process had worked successfully.

"Well I think we get the gist of things?" states the Colonel, "and it's not a pretty picture!"

"But what has all that got to do with me?" I ask apprehensively.

The Colonel looks down and holds his head in his hands while the white coats turn away. Dr Zoburg breaks the silence;

"She clearly isn't the right material Sir!"

"Now don't jump the gun Doctor, there's more we have to explain," the Colonel says staring at me directly, "You see, I'll give it to you straight, Soldier - we want you to go forward to that time in order to bring something important back to this time line."

They all nod in agreement but I stand up, not understanding the statement, querying the Colonel's request, asking him to slowly repeat it.

"So let me get this right Colonel, you want me to time travel forward to 2090 then return to our time line and bring something important back?"

"Yes, you got it Soldier!" he responds enthusiastically clapping his hands.

"I'm sorry, I don't get it! How important is important?" I probe.

"United States of America President important!" The Colonel announces standing to attention.

I want to laugh. The whole situation is absurd and I shake my head in disbelief. "No, no! Sorry, I can't - I won't do it!" I say angrily, turning to walk away from the ridiculous idea.

"Wait, wait, you haven't heard the full details. You might change your mind!" the Colonel urges. I sit down warily. I am willing to listen to the rest of the details, if only because I am curious to know what or who is so important that I have to risk my life? The white coats look relieved and resume their attentive interest, wondering how I will react.

"So go ahead Colonel, convince me, why should I undertake the mission?"

He nods and presses another button on the control panel and the 3D screens lead us into a different scene. The Colonel states, "It is the same year-2090 and there are many children lost and left without anyone to care for them. Those who are caught are taken to compounds where they are given food and shelter. Those over the age of six years have to work doing menial, repetitive tasks to earn their keep. Take a look for yourself."

The 3D screens zoom inside one such compound where a little black girl is sitting alone playing with two stones she has found in the dusty playground. Her tattered, grey uniform dress is filthy, her hair is matted and infested with lice and her eye lashes are gluey with sticky white discharge. A boy runs past laughing and hits her on the head with a broom. Tears well up in her pretty, sore eyes but she doesn't cry. She is hungry but she doesn't moan. Her little world inside her head is all she has. A knife twists in my stomach. I recognise so much of the little girl in me and feel her pain. Children like her were the reason I dedicated my life's work to protecting children. The sight of the little girl fills me with anguish, stirring up memories I wish to forget, inciting me to fight for her. The Colonel knows this and is clearly pleased his tactic is working, saying: "She is a very special child. Her father is a famous black football star and her mother a well-known white, Swedish actress. When she was born neither of them had time for her and left her in the care of a friend, who unfortunately died from a drug overdose and the child was taken to the compound. She doesn't know anything other than compound life, which is tough."

"But what can I do and why me?" I ask.

"As I said, we want you to go forwards to 2090 to bring her back to this timeline."

"Surely you have someone better suited to the task than me?"

"Physically yes! But you have a compassionate, protective, loving, motherly instinct and experience as a teacher. You are the one to bring her back to our time."

I am quiet. I want to help but there is so much at stake and I am not sure I have the confidence to tackle the assignment.

"If you accept the job you will have to be rebirthed," the Doctor states solemnly, "it is the only way you will be able to cope with the exhaustive physical demands of the illicit time travel machine and the task of retrieving a small child from captivity."

"That's true!" echoes the Colonel.

"But why do I have to endure the terrifying experience of the illicit teleporter, can't I just be brought back by a government machine?"

"That's not possible. The government in 2090 is run solely by computerised Robots and they would not understand or allow the use of their equipment for such a mundane exercise. Their time machines are used for high profile assignments and not for transporting a commoner and a little girl of no consequence back to – in their opinion, a primitive time zone."

"What is her name?"

"For now she is known as Marta."

"Marta," I repeat slowly," but why is she so important?"

"She will be our first Black Woman President of the United States of America! Think yourself lucky Soldier to be chosen to be the one to save her."

"But what if I don't bring her back?" I ask tentatively.

"Well, the future is always fan-shaped and many different avenues are open to all of us but one way or another America will have its first black woman President and we want to make sure the right woman is chosen."

"You mean there is more than one candidate for the Presidency?"

"Soldier, you are so naïve at times! Of course there's more than one candidate there's always more than one lined up for every important post in the world. The powers that be decide on who they groom and prime for the Presidency. Remember we can't change fate, but we can make improvements along the way".

I nod, experiencing a whole gamut of emotions. I am surprised, delighted, scared, apprehensive, and uncertain about the task.

"Look Soldier, you will be fine. We'll re-birth you, get you fit for the job and in no time you'll be back with the cargo. You'll be lucky, first time round."

"You mean others have failed?" I gasp.

"I didn't say that I just said you'll be lucky."

Yes I will be lucky, for I am Lucky and I will try my best to bring her back.

MIND OVER MATTER

The enormous responsibility of the assignment ahead is daunting and my mind is reeling with questions and doubts, but most of all I fear the worst - what if I get killed?

"Well I guess that's all for now," the Colonel says, "you will of course be fully prepared for the operation and all your queries will be answered in due course."

"I need a drink!" I exclaim.

"Give the woman a drink!" he laughs, "and let her eat whatever she wants Doctor. She deserves a treat!"

Dr Zoburg nods disdainfully and exits, returning a few moments later with a full drinks tray which she places disapprovingly on a small table.

"That's right soldier, enjoy yourself before we begin to prepare you, in earnest, for the interesting hard times ahead."

Holding up a glass of bubbly to salute the Colonel as he disappears I wallow in the delight of the champagne bubbles popping up my nose.

The white coat team evaporate as the sitting room reverts to its quaint disguise and I settle down to my welcome drink with Freddie at my feet by the lovely bright fire. There is so much to think about and assimilate before embarking on a dangerous assignment from which there is no guarantee that I will return safely, with the precious cargo. I wonder how long I have before the training begins. I pour myself another glass of sparkling wine, sinking into the comfy chair with relief, happy that the gruelling physical work-out has been cancelled. The Colonel said I could eat whatever I wished and I have a sudden urge to look in the fridge to see what treats I am allowed. I am not disappointed as all my favourite food is neatly stored and labelled and chocolate bars of chocolaty- chocolate are temptingly stacked on the bottom shelf. I greedily rip off the wrapper of a fruit and nut bar, gorging on the sheer indulgence of a chocolate feast.

A few days go by in isolated peace and undiluted gastronomic heaven, eating and drinking whatever and whenever I want, in-between taking wonderful country walks with Freddie, then unashamedly flopping in front of a sizzling fire and drifting lazily into the evening watching my favourite films on a cine-screen. I wallow in forgotten melodies of romantic music, and lose myself in classical symphonies, indulging my desire to wander into adventurous, imagined landscapes with the passion of a sentenced prisoner about to meet their death.

But now, where is the now? I am sitting on a rock gazing across a magnificent Welsh valley with Freddie by my side. The air is crisp and clean like a pure mountain stream bubbling over stones, rippling through gullies and cascading into clear pools of fresh water. I am grateful to be in the moment, living the life-force itself and thankful to know nature again before the planet becomes a dusty desert. As I sit watching birds glide on the warm air currents below, fear begins to creep into my thoughts and doubt trickles through cracks in my surety. Suspicion springboards from one certainty to another, taunting, teasing, debilitating, eating into my confidence and tearing away all security. I begin to distrust, suspect, disbelieve and hesitate about the safety of the forthcoming mission. I try to force all my misgivings into a deep pit, but the chasm grows wider into a quarry of despair and the more I attempt to dig myself out, the more I fall into the quicksand of despondency. I gaze beyond the shimmering trees and call for help to the Great Ones of the Universe and my whisperers answer my call saying:

"You terrify yourself with destructive thoughts and allow your mind to take over, believing that the little negative voice in your head is you, but it isn't! You trust in your beliefs which you think you form yourself but it is a trick, a lie that all humans accept as truth. Not all thoughts are your own!"

"But if I don't initiate my thoughts, who does?" I question, confused by the implications. A single voice like a silver bell tinkling in the breeze answers; *"Ah, my little friend you have much to learn. You trust in your judgement and what your mind tells you, but your understanding of the greater picture is infinitesimally small. Humans are like tiny microbes on a grain of sand in the desert in comparison to powerful, superior forces in a teeming cosmos brimming with higher life forms."*

It is difficult to imagine the notion of humanity's insignificance in a universe of multi, multi-verses and it is humbling to know that our level of intellect is inconsequential to other beings of higher intelligence. The delicate voice hears my thoughts and continues:

"Yes, all this is hard for you to grasp and harder still to realise that superior, higher beings created humans as a kind of experiment, aiming to use the homo sapiens as slaves for their needs, but giving the species the ability to procreate and increase in number to relieve the superiors of the tedious task."

I am disturbed by this information and walk on towards a disused slate quarry, mulling over the idea of being created by powerful entities and not by the Master of Masters. My whisperers hear my thoughts and sigh in unison answering my question as one voice:

"The Great Master of Masters is the source essence of One, the Almighty of All that is, was and forever will be. Your mind cannot imagine this phenomenon because you do not have the brain power to comprehend the concept."

An eerie wind whines through the trees and a buzzing sensation lifts my consciousness to receive further enlightenment:

"You wonder why the Father of All Being could allow superior beings to create humans as slaves, well, you see, the earth is a unique planet where the inhabitants have the capacity to make choices. They can select who they want to be, where they wish to

be and how to conduct their lives. This choice dictates their ability to generate their own inner energy, which is their soul's vibration and the strength of this internal vigour determines the level of their spiritual progress".

I begin to understand the teaching, but still question why the Great One allowed the creation of humans by Aliens, but before I ask the question a gentle voice responds:

"Because of the 'choice' element, all beings have free will to decide their own pathway and because of this premise, superior beings were allowed to create humans, but a stipulation was made by the Great One to instil into homo-sapiens a hidden, secret energy unique to each individual. Soul energy was the ingredient directly sourced from the Great One, connecting the human directly to the Source of all Being, which means the true essence of all humanity will never die and the pure Soul Vibration of LOVE sets the human apart from all other species."

"Yes, of course 'Love', I add, pausing to listen further:

"The ruling Superior Aliens created the human body with a limited lifespan so that the body would die after a certain amount of time in service, while the addition of the 'soul' meant that the spirit lives on eternally, giving humans 'soul power' birthed from the Source of all Source. Humans, with their ability to love and feel emotions, are unique and other species who do not have this gift are curious about its power. Remember love is all. Love is the key to everything."

The wind whistles through the trees and an ancient iron gate creaks in the old slate quarry, echoing a solitary grinding whinge across the strange landscape. The voice inside my head begins to fade as the last streaks of bright sunshine fall behind a cloud and I hear:

"With 'love' humans are able to elevate themselves above all other beings. That is why other species envy the humans and want to steal DNA to create hybrids."

The voice folds into the void and I feel the truth of the message, knowing within my heart that the information is correct. My whisperer's message empowers me and an inner strength rises as I arrive at the dilapidated quarry gateway. Freddie looks at me sideways, questioning whether I ought to venture into such a strange place. I pause to investigate an old sign hanging precariously from a rusty iron pole. The faded letters still threaten caution: 'Private Property. Keep out. Trespassers will be prosecuted by order of Thomas J. Williams Owner'. I smile as I step across the decayed, rotten gate not heeding the warning and into the long-abandoned site. I imagine the noise of the work force that existed inside such a male bastion, where men worked hard for a pittance to provide for their families. Now the world has robots!

I am alone with Freddie trotting by my side, in a strange stone world where mounds of unused slate lie, untouched for centuries, honed by skilled men who knew how to quarry, cut, sculpt and build beautiful homes, creating artefacts from the earth's crust. The old sign creaks a melancholy cracked melody behind us as we venture farther into a moonscape of extreme shapes and textures, embellished by nature's constant handiwork. Little hollows and crevices, overgrown with weeds and bracken, lie hidden in angular rocks and statues fashioned by the wind stand tall in a metamorphic slate paradise. Ancient minerals colour the slate in a myriad of hues - grey, blue, purple and green - such a rainbow array of dull lustred colours uniquely decorate extreme textures of ragged, knife-sharp ridges to smooth-topped, slippery boulders set in a pre-historic amphitheatre.

Freddie runs on ahead and finds a small cave, like a mystical grotto, concealed amongst the tall ferns and I am wary of disturbing snakes sleeping in crevices. As I creep inside where there is just enough light to trace magical cyan patterns formed in the rock, like antediluvian cave drawings, tiny twinkles of gold sparkle farther up the rock face, too high to reach, taunting the eye with wondrous beauty, like precious golden jewellery hidden in Egyptian tombs. Here, eras are timeless and meaningless in the abandoned slate kingdom. The song of the underworld is dark and mysterious, accompanied by the slow echo of spring water dripping down hidden fissures. In the deep stillness the birds sing. Inside the enchanting den, I imagine lovers' clandestine meetings and furtive coven rituals performed by moonlight.

Suddenly a bird shrieks from a nearby tree shaking me free from my fantasies and Freddie bounds outside while I follow, scrambling back into the rocky realm where, ungainly, like a child, I clamber up a large, blue-grey boulder and stand on the top looking out across the unfamiliar landscape where dinosaurs once roamed. I spy a large tree with its centre core cut in two by lightning, the old bark still showing burnt streaks from the attack and yet, sprouting from the dead half, new shoots appear awakening the lifeless wood in re-birth. I smile at nature's round of birth-life-death and take comfort in the thought that after the cold, dark winter, bright sunny daffodils and fresh spring buds regenerate the earth with new beginnings. Freddie, not wanting to leave my side, finds a little path up through the scree and sits next to me on the top of the boulder. I love his faithful vigilance, but a strange thought creeps into my mind - maybe he was sent to spy on me? I dismiss the idea as he is so loving and I can't accept the fact that he might be a tracking device relaying back to the commander all my actions. I love him just the way he is and I dismiss the thought as my mind wanders to the appliances and gadgets of the world today.

I sigh into the breeze blowing across the boulders, contemplating the future obsession with human regeneration and am fearful of the process I have to undergo to succeed in my assignment. I fear the unknown trials ahead and seek solace from my long-term friend Yuli, a Buddhist monk, who helped to heal me many years ago, from a debilitating sickness. I sit on the top of the smooth rock with Freddie tucked in close and shut my eyes, breathing deeply, allowing a higher vibration to access my mind. A welcome, friendly voice greets me:

"You have many questions, my dear friend."

Yuli stands before me in his yellow and orange robes smiling his infectious grin. He is small in stature but has the strength of a lion and the gentleness of a dove. Swiftly, without action, he sits beside me stating:

"You make everything seem so complicated in here!" He says softly, tapping my forehead. "There is nothing that cannot be tamed by 'love'. You know love is like the all- purpose cleaning spray-it is good for everything!" he laughs nodding his head.

I smile. He always has a practical, down-to-earth way of looking at life.

"You see you forget that this body of yours is only a vessel - you know the milk bottle will not nourish you, only the milk inside will satisfy your needs. So too, it is not your body that will transcend the material world, only your soul. You must find sustenance for your soul's well-being."

I understand, and say "I can't stop these negative thoughts and worries about what I have to do!"

"Then don't do it!" He replies, curtly.

I pause, not expecting his reply and say, "but I want to!"

"Then why are you going round and round in circles, like a dog chasing his tail? Is it not a good deed you are going to do?"

"Yes." I reply, meekly.

"Then all will be well, as all is well. Do not trouble me whining like a baby. All things tackled with good intentions will come good. Good intentions are your life jacket in the storm."

"But...?"

"Do what you have to do and do it with a good trusting heart, or don't do it all. Which child wins the song contest? Not the one with the best voice, but the one with the smiley face!"

I hug him and he disappears into the ether. I know he will always hear my plea for help wherever he is in the Universe and his wise words show me a deeper insight into myself and I resolve to tackle the oncoming challenges with a good heart. I stand and Freddie is relieved to be making a move as the sun is sinking fast behind the mountains and the light is dimming, creating murky shadows behind the shapes that appeared beautiful earlier, but are now dark and menacing. Grim statues morph into grotesque gargoyles that leer at me as I scurry past grey tombstones, left stacked in blocks in the long grass. Eerie creeks and cracking sounds ricochet off the rock face as it cools and contracts in the chilly evening and I wish I hadn't stayed so long in the enchanting kingdom. Freddie jumps up at me, urging me to move faster as he too senses the sinister mood change and with pounding heart I pick up the pace, wishing I was fitter and able to run faster. My mind hurtles back to a time, when, as a small child I was haunted by night terrors. Nightly, my bedroom was invaded by half-eaten faces decaying and rotting in graves, staring up at me calling for help. At the time I had no notion that my house was built on an ancient Druid burial site and nightly I found myself stepping over and in between anguished corpses pleading with me to save them. It was an inferno of lost souls and all I could do was scream and scream until my parents came. They always thought it was only nightmares, but I knew it wasn't!

Being very young I was still very close to my own people from another world and I was taught some lessons to help me cope with my psychic gifts. My secret force would teach me how to concentrate and drive my mind to focus on other things, knowing that when the mind is distracted, focus shifts, alleviating fear. They took me into a black tunnel where there was a tiny dot of light at the end. My mission was to go through the tunnel fixing my mind on the minute spec, not paying attention to the dark but keeping a watch on the light, which, as I moved forwards grew bigger and bigger until I was standing in a beam of bright white light. They taught me that when the brain forces the mind to fixate on one purpose, the mind forgets fear and deals only with the task in hand. They explained that the mind is powerful enough to overcome all material obstacles and that the lesson was important because I would need to use the practice many times in my life. They were right because a few nights later I had need to use the technique.

Living in a small agricultural village, farm and dairy produce was easily available directly from the farms and my mother sent me out on a dark winter's night to buy eggs. I was afraid of the dark and didn't want to go, but fear of my mother's wrath was greater. I ran to the other end of the village and despite the lateness of the hour, the farmer's wife was very friendly and gave me half a dozen eggs in a brown cardboard carton. As soon as I left the farm heavy rain pelted the earth, turning the dry ground into a sea of mud. I wasn't wearing a coat and was drenched in seconds. Suddenly the air stilled and the sky rumbled and the ground shook. Overhead, a pink, electric shock wave streaked the sky with firefly flashes of lightning bolts bombing the heavens. I was terrified. I ran and ran not heeding the dark or where I was going until I reached a house that had always fascinated me. It belonged to a family of musicians, the father was a well-known conductor. I stood under the shelter of their beautiful trees for a few moments, wondering how I had got there as my house was in the opposite direction at the other end of the village. I was frightened and began to panic, clutching the box of eggs to my chest and then I remembered my mind lesson. If I looked at the tiny spec of light and didn't take any notice of the dark around me I would reach home safely. So I braced myself, ready to dash through the pelting rain, racing through the dark streets, keeping the light of my own home in my mind.

Eventually I turned a corner and the lights of my house welcomed me back. My mother was in the kitchen with her back to me as I entered and asked if I had the eggs. I told her I had them but when she turned around she grimaced. I was dripping wet and the eggs were plastered to my dress. Egg yolks and sticky white slime dripped from the cardboard box and from my long hair. Pools of water dripped onto her clean kitchen floor. In my fear and panic I had crushed the eggs unknowingly to my chest. She didn't scold me because I think she felt guilty for sending me out late in the dark and just took the messy carton and tried to salvage some of the yolk still slopping in the bottom. I remember the incident well as it was an early 'mind over matter' experience which was a forerunner of many more, later in my life.

The memory fades as Freddie and I race back to the cottage and I am relieved to see the lights beaming a greeting in the dark. As I open the door I am startled to find a noisy reception. The white coat team, the Doctor, Lee Wan Chu, Serdonis and the Colonel are busy discussing something.

"Ah, come in Soldier, we are discussing our course of action for you," the Colonel says in an unusually friendly manner. I smile awkwardly and take off my coat. As I sit down in my armchair I notice a large mosquito bite on my right wrist which itches irritatingly and I begin to scratch it. The Doctor notices and takes my arm to examine it.

"You have to be careful of the mosquitoes around here, they are a particular species with a voracious appetite for human flesh and can give you a nasty infection. Let me put some ointment on that," she says and disappears.

"Yes, mosquitoes? Who would have thought from such a tiny creature encapsulated in a piece of amber, scientists would extract its DNA to make the most fascinating discovery…" "That's enough Serdonis, we haven't got time for all of that right now!" the Doctor snaps, applying medicated cream to my wrist.

"Well, you are lucky having such a great team to take care of you Soldier!" laughs the Colonel.

I smile, thinking 'of course I am lucky, because I am LUCKY!'

REBIRTHING vs REGENERATION

I am disappointed to find the welcome committee waiting for me, as I had been looking forward to spending the evening alone by the fire with Freddie, indulging in my favourite wine and watching an old film but I realise any chance of that special time is now over and I have to begin preparations for the assignment.

"Well soldier. Let's jump straight in. You agreed it would be best to re-birth you, reclaiming you at around the age of twenty-five years, or thereabouts - is that correct?" enquires the Colonel.

I nod and bite my lip, I feel nauseous about the whole affair.

"We are going to take you to the centre for 'rebirthing' and show you exactly how it's done. Please feel free to ask any questions along the way," adds the Colonel.

I nod as we are drawn into a techno-conversion of the cottage as it transforms into a massive, dimly lit warehouse where the ceiling is completely indiscernible with layers upon layers and rows upon rows of clear, oval vessels containing naked human bodies suspended in transparent fluid that hang from steel rods. We stand quietly around the doctor as she explains:

"Each body is kept in stasis at different stages and ages of development from the foetus to babies and toddlers, teenagers and to fully-grown adults."

The scene is both grotesque and fascinating and I am uncomfortable thinking that one of those naked bodies hanging in a pod might soon be me! The doctor continues:

"The atmosphere is designed to imitate a womb-like environment for the developing human and each casket is labelled at the age and stage at which the person is to be brought out of stasis and be re-born into the world."

"What happens before this state is induced, I mean, how do you er...I mean how will you...?"

"How do we put you in stasis?" the doctor asks.

"Yes," I reply, subdued by my rising anxiety and the shock of seeing thousands of suspended bodies.

"Good question and a good question deserves a detailed answer," interrupts Serdonis, helpfully.

"If you don't mind Serdonis," the doctor says firmly, "all her questions will be fully answered. Now please follow me."

We follow her respectfully like shadows passing through rows of floating bodies into a brightly lit elevator that descends into a white clinical basement, where doctors in white coats, holding delicate instruments walk purposefully to operating theatres.

"This is stage one," the Doctor halts outside a security-locked door where, as she uses retinal identification, the door slides open to admit us to a white waiting area. "We will be allowed to watch the first stage of the process through the studio windows. Follow me."

Following the doctor, we enter a small theatre with three tiers of seats where everyone can view the operation through a thick perspex window. Below are two doctors and three nurses masked and gowned ready to begin. The surgeon gives a nod to Doctor Zoburg and she nods back. A door opens and a man in a white operating gown walks in and is escorted to what appears to be similar to a dentist's chair with instruments and lights attached. The surgeon slides his mask down over his mouth and addresses us, giving us the details of the operation he is about to perform.

"Welcome ladies and gentlemen. The procedure I am about to perform is called 'Transference'. The human form or container is designed with an engine - the 'brain'. The brain is a tremendously powerful machine which is capable of much more than humans realise because, on the whole, they do not explore its full potential. They are lazy and only use approximately five per cent of the brain's capacity, routinely relying on its automatic mode. The brain, in fact, has up to eleven different dimensions and in some cases more, especially if the human has psychic abilities."

He pauses then begins again – "Now back to the task in hand. First we have to put this sleeve, or vessel into a cryo-sleep," he gestures to the man in the seat who is smiling up at the doctor. "You will note, no nasty injections, just a simple fruit drink, will place the subject into a deep, deep sleep."

We watch as the man is given a small glass containing a light pink liquid which he drinks and with the effect almost immediate, he falls into a deep sleep. The second doctor demonstrates that the subject is completely sedated, by sliding a large needle into the top of the man's head without any sign of a response from the subject. "Now we are going to extract some cells from the brain in order to grow a new younger brain, whilst still maintaining the unique individuality and personality of the subject," the surgeon says as he stands to one side while the other doctor withdraws the needle containing a red fluid which he seals into a metal ampoule.

"The brain cells will now begin a new journey of re-growth in our lab," the doctor adds.

"But what if they get the cells mixed up with someone else's?" I question, panicking, plagued with doubts. The doctor pre-empts my query and assures us that it is not possible to give another body someone else's brain as every living cell, membrane and organ is DNA aligned and the body would reject any intruder that did not match up to the subject's DNA. I am reassured by his explanation and wait to see the next stage of the process. "The next stage ladies and gentlemen is the transference of the mind computer system. You see the 'brain' is the Captain of the ship and the main engine that drives the vessel and the 'mind' is the navigator directing the driving dynamism. I should explain that the human was created as part of an Independent Force controlled by its creators, through a computerised mechanism connected to a high-powered computer grid. Every human mind is connected to the Universal grid of knowledge. The human mind is, itself, an advanced computer with the ability to think for itself and to reject the external 'mind control' cuckoo thoughts that can invade the mind and take over the subject, emanating from the external, main computer."

"My whisperers were trying to explain this to me and now I know why some thoughts are interlopers into our minds," I whisper to Serdonis who nods in agreement and is about to enlighten me with his compendium of knowledge when the surgeon continues:

"So as the 'mind' is a complex computer we have to be careful to extract it as a working machine. However, sometimes the memory vortex is distorted during the operation and the subject may not always recover their past life memories."

We watch fascinated, as a helmet enmeshed with a myriad of pink wires descends from a mechanism attached to the back of the couch and is placed on the head of the subject. The main lights dim as the doctors and nurses stand back from the buzzing helmet as it whizzes into action, whirring with circular purple lights around the subject's head. This process lasts a few minutes until the beams slowly dim and disappear. Then a small device, containing all the extracted mind information is placed into a small, square, steel box, and we are told, will be transferred to another lab.

"So ladies and gentlemen we have two major components of the human body extracted and ready to be reinstalled at a later date - the brain and the mind which work together as a team. Now we are left with the most precious element that a human possesses which is of course...the 'soul' or the main dynamic energy which can never be destroyed. This energy is like an electric current which passes through the body and stays encapsulated in the vessel until the body wears out and dies."

I am engrossed in the doctor's lecture and demonstration and am eager to know how soul transference works in practice. I have known about the employment of the procedure for many years, a procedure which has been used by royalty as far back as the Egyptian pharaohs and has been well documented by top scientists many times since.

"There are two main exits and entrances which the soul energy utilizes at birth and death," explains the doctor," one is in the middle of the forehead, often referred to as the 'third eye' and is situated opposite the pineal gland. The other is at the back of the neck and is also close to the pineal gland. The pineal gland has been described as the 'seat of the soul' and acts as a doorway for the spirit to enter and exit a body."

"What if the pineal gland is calcified?" I ask the doctor, who nods.

"Good question, good question that needs a specific answer," adds Serdonis.

"Serdonis, please, we have everything under control!" The doctor says pointedly as she raises her hand and directs my question to the surgeon who answers promptly.

"Yes, if the pineal gland is calcified it can cause problems whilst the body is in living mode and can cause a subject to change their sleep patterns. It can disorientate a person or cause Alzheimer's disease. Calcification is often caused by fluoride intake."

"Ah! So that's why the powers that be flooded the market with fluoride products, especially toothpaste! It was meant to prevent tooth decay but was obviously a ruse to destroy human enlightenment through the pineal gland!" I retort. The doctor is not pleased with my outburst and requests my full attention.

"Calcification of the pineal gland does not affect the soul's exit and at pre-birth it is a healthy organ not yet sullied by the outside world. To extract the electric soul energy we take a powerful, electrical suction machine." He holds up a small tool that looks rather like a miniature hoover with a long nozzle on one end and a sealed perspex tube on the other, "and apply it, like so, to the forehead or back of the neck. In this case we will use the third eye point."

We watch, spell-bound, as a bright yellow hazy mist is drawn out of the forehead and sucked into the tube where it emits a luminescent glow and is transferred to a silver capsule. There, it is sealed to be stored in the lab. The surgeon explains that the light emanating from the soul varies from person to person according to the strength of the inner energy generated through their life experiences. "And there you have it ladies and gentlemen-soul transference," the surgeon says, pulling off his surgical gloves.

"But how did you learn the procedure?" I enquire.

"Good question, very good question, deserves an answer," interjects Serdonis.

Doctor Zoburg directs an angry glare at Serdonis and allows my question to be put forward to the surgeon.

"Whatever can be placed into a container can be taken out with a reverse process," maintains the surgeon." You see, the higher Alien beings with their vast superior knowledge when creating humans were ordered, from the highest Source, to place a soul inside each creature to make it unique unto itself. Obviously then, knowledge of how to implant a soul into a human body is tantamount to extracting it," he declares victoriously, shaking off his mask and operating gown to reveal his silver Alien body and striking elongated head. Amazingly, he is one of the Aliens who had a hand in creating humans and is proud to demonstrate his awe inspiring knowledge and skill.

"Thank you for allowing us to watch the fascinating operation," the doctor says as she gathers us all together for our next viewing. The Alien surgeon nods and disappears.

The Colonel who has been silent throughout the lecture takes me to one side while the others follow the doctor down the corridor asking;

"Ok soldier, are you alright with all of this so far?"

"Yes sir." I reply meekly.

"That's fine then because next we are going to witness body shrinkage in preparation for foetal regrowth. You have to see this in order to understand what is going to happen to you."

"Yes sir." I gulp, as I reply.

"Look Soldier, I have seen on the battlefield, in a region on Mars for example, men half-eaten by six feet tall spiders and left to die in agony, but with our fantastic scientific knowledge put into practice in our state-of-the-art clinics, the half-eaten men have re-grown limbs, torsos and even almost full bodies in no time at all. Trust me?"

"Yes sir." I reply with a stubborn lump in my throat making me almost inaudible.

"Well let's jump to it then, Soldier. Onward and upward!" he laughs as he slaps my back encouragingly.

We find the others seated around a large, clinical, white table, edged with gullies designed to catch excess fluid dripping from bodies. Dr Zoburg motions us to our allotted seats and we wait for the 'shrinking' procedure to begin. The lights fade as though we are about to watch a theatrical performance and two scientists walk in, accompanied by an assistant. The scientists in white coats stand at each side of the table as a naked body covered with a white cloth is wheeled in on a trolley. Two assistants lift the body off the trolley onto the table and quickly exit. The lights soften again almost into darkness as an overhead steel robot folds down over the subject. The scientists roll down the cover to the patient's shoulders revealing the head of a beautiful young girl with long curly auburn hair. I gasp in surprise as I hadn't expected such a young, lovely person to be laid out on the table. I imagine myself in her place and shudder. I am afraid to watch but make myself focus on the table because I need to know what is going to happen to me, however gruesome.

"Friends, this is Rosaria who has chosen to be rebirthed as a new-born, due to the health reasons she has suffered in her young life. She will be taken right back to foetal status where she will grow and develop again, free from the congenital disease which she inherited. The body is only a corpse at this stage, as the brain, mind and soul have already been removed and are in storage awaiting re-processing. But first, we will remove the heart."

I wince at the thought and feel sick, but at the same time, I am mesmerized by the process. The other scientist flicks a switch and the surgeon robot rotates a sharp instrument around the heart area which slices neatly through the skin. The organ is lifted out in one deft move, without damaging any cells.

"The heart has memory cells like the brain and has up to fifteen different memory channels. Therefore people with heart transplants are very likely to experience memories from their donors. As you have been informed the brain is the engine that commands the ship, the mind the navigator, so the heart is the fuel which fires both mechanisms. Preserving the heart of the subject in question is very important," adds the scientist pointing to the live organ, beating in the robot's clutch. "You will note that the heart is still alive but the rest of the body is dead. We have a method of keeping the heart beating so that when it is removed from the body we can keep it alive in a saline solution until it is placed back into the subject's body. It will then be reduced in size ready for the time it has to be accommodated in a baby's body."

The assistant respectfully takes the heart and places it in a golden box which is taken to the lab for storage. The next process happens very quickly and two procedures occur simultaneously, so it is very hard to distinguish which instrument is responsible for what action.

"Now the body will be reduced back to foetal status."

We watch as the robot takes a larger, longer instrument, like a very fine sword and begins slicing in a circular motion around the body removing skin and bone. Blood pours into the gullies and at the same time an overhead square machine like a cine projector, runs a film of the subject's life backwards, until we see a tiny fish-like foetus lying on the table. The assistant carefully places the minute being into a small Perspex pod and takes it away to hang in the development zone.

I need air. I feel faint. I can't believe what I have just witnessed! This brutality, performed in a scientific, clinical operating theatre is disgusting, yet it will give the girl a new lease of life. The Colonel sees my distress and quickly takes me out into the corridor where he makes me sit down and orders an assistant to bring me a glass of water.

"Ok Soldier? I know viewing all this for the first time is distressing, but it's progress."

I feel dizzy and not sure whether I want to continue the tour and uncertain whether I even dare to attempt the mission after seeing what is involved.

"Feeling better Soldier?" The Colonel sounds sympathetic.

I nod and finish the drink of water.

"Right, well there's just one more procedure to view and that is the actual birthing process itself."

The Colonel helps me up and we walk over to the rest of the group who are waiting outside a blue door with the letters BIRTHING written on it boldly, in black.

The doctor introduces us to the Matron Midwife, Mrs Macoy, who explains that near to the birthing time the client is taken for 'Transference treatment', which means their major organs are reinstalled to their bodies and the brain, mind and soul are transferred back. This can happen at any age or stage whether pre-natal, ante-natal or grown adult.

"The final process you are about to witness is very special, as the client is re-born into the world and will have a new birth date."

"Happy birthday! Happy birthday!" pipes up Serdonis who is immediately halted from further interruption by a savage look from Doctor Zoburg.

"Quite!" smiles Mrs Macoy politely, "if you would like to follow me and take a seat."

We enter a small waiting room with a few seats placed next to a large window where we can view the whole operation. The operating room is small, painted blue from floor to ceiling and looks like a walk–in wet room with deep gullies entrenched around the edges to catch excess water. Two men enter, clad in blue waterproof gear from head to toe. A woman enters who we are told is the presiding midwife. She is also dressed in splash-proof clothing.

"Our new-born is an adult man and so we have two male nurse assistants presiding over the operation. If our new-born is a girl or a woman, then our birthing assistants are female," Mrs Macoy explains.

I watch the two men hose down the tiled floor and note they have the physiques of security guards.

"You will note that our male nurses also double as security guards as sometimes, especially when an adult male is re-birthed, sometimes a client can be violent and may have an aggressive reaction to the process," explains Mrs Macoy.

"Why?" I ask, puzzled by her statement.

"At present, we are not entirely certain why this reaction occurs, so we are doing extensive research into this aspect of re-birthing to ensure a one hundred per cent tranquil entry. I have to inform you of this just in case our client today has an adverse reaction. I don't want you to be alarmed by the restraining techniques applied by the guards, sorry I mean nurses."

"Are the female er... nurses also security guards?" I ask.

"That is correct and now we must move on as the client is about to enter," Mrs Macoy says hastily.

The back wall has a large, curtained opening with blue plastic flaps like the luggage reclaim bays in airports. A mechanised railway track runs from the birthing suite to the collection point. Suddenly the flaps flutter like little flags and a large pod trundles in along the tracks, shaped like a large oyster shell full of clear fluid and containing a naked, male body floating peacefully in the water. When the pod stops in the centre of the room the midwife flicks a switch and the fluid rapidly drains out of the shell. When all the liquid has evaporated, the lid rises and the two birthing nurses step forwards placing their hands on the sides of the cot. The midwife puts breathing apparatus over the client's face which encourages him to take his first reborn breath. We watch closely as his chest begins to rise and fall and his eyes open wide. He sits up shakily, uncertain of his surroundings. The lights dim and soft, peaceful music plays. The assistants help him out of the pod and hose him down to clean away a sticky white, waxy substance that has protected his body during the waiting time. They wrap him in a towel. The man, around thirty years of age seems calm and placid and happy for the assistants to lead him to a wheelchair where he is wheeled out to face the world as a new man. Mrs Macoy seems relieved and sighs. She says she hopes we enjoyed the viewing, but as she speaks, the back flaps flutter again and another pod glides in.

"I'm sorry this is most unusual to have another re-birth so soon, I think we should go?" She seems flustered.

But it is too late to usher us out as the next birthing process is activated. Two strong women nurses rush in gowned and booted for the process. The midwife in charge seems even more flustered as the nurse's exchange glances when the pod halts before them. The water drains and the nurses edge forwards gripping onto the side of the pod with clenched fists. Mrs Macoy receives an emergency call and swiftly leaves the room. The administering Midwife places the breathing apparatus over the woman's mouth and we watch her chest rise and fall. She is about twenty-five years of age with a shaved head and strong angular features, in fact her whole body appears very masculine. She opens her sharp blue eyes and stares at the ceiling, then she looks down at her body - and screams, jumping out of the pod slipping and sliding over the floor, hitting out at everything in sight. She throws a punch at the midwife and sends her crashing against the wall where she hits her head on a metal instrument. The midwife flops down as blood gushes from her head and spills over the floor. The naked rebirth subject thrashes out at another of the nurses but misses and the other acts swiftly to plunge a syringe into her back which sedates her, almost immediately. The two nurses pick up the body and dump it into a wheelchair and whisk her away. A doctor enters the unit and tends to the injured midwife as a guard comes into our watch room and ushers us out where Mrs Macoy waits apologetically, ready to explain the terrible assault.

"Oh dear, I am so, so sorry that you had to witness that!"

"It happens," the Colonel says, matter of factly, but please elucidate and explain matters to my company here."

"Yes Colonel indeed, again I am so sorry that you had to watch that brutal attack. That process is part of one of the extra services we offer the government."

"The Judiciary?" the Colonel asks.

"Yes sir. That woman was previously a man. He was a serial murderer and raped many women. The Judge ruled that he be rebirthed as a woman and let out into the criminal world to take his punishment," she explains.

I nod, I understand now why the rebirthing subject was so angry when she woke up.

"Is that punishment actually legal?" I ask, genuinely shocked.

"Indeed it is and there are many more aspects to the birthing system that I cannot, at present, reveal."

"Thank you Mrs Macoy, you have been most helpful," declares Dr Zoburg as she escorts us out to the lift.

We are all silent, even Serdonis is quiet as we return to the main foyer. The doctor and the Colonel huddle together in private discussion about something and then the Colonel takes me to one side while the others depart.

"Look Soldier, you are going to spend the night here in the centre and you can think about things and let us know in the morning what you have decided, ok?"

All I can think about in that moment is whether Freddie is alright and ask, "Who is going to take care of Freddie?"

The Colonel smiles and whispers, "he's a cyber- pet, remember?" and with that he walks away leaving me in shock, to ponder the situation.

A few minutes later a lady assistant takes my arm and walks me to a long corridor with rows of white doors, which I assume are hospitality rooms for patients. My assumption is correct as she unlocks a room and invites me to make myself comfortable, enquiring if I need anything or wish to have food brought up, but I am not hungry and I decline her offer. I am so tired and drained after the tour and I need to sleep, so I slump on to the bed and fall into a deep sleep. The next morning I wake up to the clattering sound of a breakfast tray being laid on a small table next to my bed. A young, friendly assistant tells me that after breakfast I have a meeting in the board room downstairs. I nod as I sit up and am grateful for the coffee and toast. Half an hour later the same assistant escorts me to the meeting room where the Colonel, Dr Zoburg and a scientist wait, ready with their reports.

"Come in, come in Soldier," welcomes the Colonel, "I hope you slept well and are feeling better?"

I nod as I sit down nervously at the conference table.

Dr Zoburg opens her report and states," We have all your health details and have agreed that you need not be 'rebirthed' as such but can be regenerated to the age of about twenty-five years."

"Yes, how does that sound Soldier? Better than doing the whole caboodle, hey?" laughs the Colonel.

With my head on one side I try to evaluate their suggestion as I wonder what to say.

"It means my dear, that you don't have to undergo any of the transference operations you witnessed yesterday or the retrograde process to foetal status, as you can be regenerated in your present form to the age required," the scientist says.

"That's great, isn't it?" enthuses the Colonel.

"So that means I don't have to go through *any* of those processes?" I ask timidly.

"Yep, you got it Soldier, so what do you say?" chirps the Colonel.

"I think that will be fine, but what does it *actually* entail?" I enquire tentatively.

"Well, we zoom you back through our Teleport time enhancer and having been a dancer, at the age of twenty-five and still dancing at that time, you will be very fit and able to complete the mission" the scientist says, assuredly.

"So let me get this right, all I have to do is be transferred back to my original age of twenty-five. Will I still have my memory?"

"You will have your memory intact up to that age, although you may get from time-to-time flashes of your future self. That is quite normal," affirms the scientist.

"You will of course undergo a short period of training for the mission, afterwards," the doctor says. I gulp remembering the last session, not relishing a repeat performance of the torture. The Colonel notes my reaction and laughs, patting me on the back and declaring:

"Relax, relax, Soldier, it's going to be fine, after all, at the age of twenty-five you'll be fit and ready for action!"

I smile, somewhat comforted by his reassurance, while the doctor impatiently shuffles from one foot to the other saying:

"Time to start things moving Sir. We're running out of time!"

"Yes, yes, of course. Well, Soldier, I'll leave you in very good hands. You'll hear from me before you go." He salutes informally and exits.

The doctor and the scientist swap notes and an assistant enters with a document for me to sign that says I agree to undertake the regeneration programme. I am given instructions to follow before the process can begin. I have to fast for 24 hours, drinking only a small amount of water in order to prepare my body for the operation. I am not allowed to mingle with anyone during the next twenty-four hours in case I am contaminated by germs or viruses and so I am assigned a comfortable room with TV and cine facilities in which to entertain myself. I am also given a short informative video of the Regeneration Programme offered by the Institute of Organic Consciousness, Dept. of Frontiers of Aging and after some thought I decide it would be a good idea to watch it, although if it changes my mind, it is too late now – I have signed the agreement contract!

The video begins with a short history of the Institute and explains new scientific advances in breakthrough techniques that conquer the frontiers of the ageing process, which I quickly skip and get to the actual procedure which takes approximately half an hour although the recovery time is much longer- roughly about two and a half hours. I watch as an old man, hardly able to walk, is assisted onto an operating table where his head is secured by a steel brace. His arms and legs are fastened to bedside rails by what appear to be fortified handcuffs, on his wrists and ankles. A white beam from an overhead machine scans his body up and down and relaxes him into a deep sleep state, whereupon a plum-red coloured capsule is lowered from the ceiling and placed over him, completely covering him in a plasma cocoon. At first a gentle light is generated inside the capsule lighting up the patient's body in a warm glow then the machine gains momentum whizzing and whirring, picking up speed as the light glows more intense. I understand, watching the process that the patient is physically restrained during the operation because of the lightning speed at which the body's cells are attacked. Suddenly the light inside the capsule disappears and the contraption glides upwards off the patient, back to its original position, leaving the subject fully regenerated at the required age. I gaze, dumbfounded at the healthy, handsome young man who now lies where the old, infirm person had been before the process. Two assistants release the restraints and wheel him out to a recovery room. I have to admit that I am very impressed by the end results and feel more confident about facing my own regeneration operation.

I wonder what it will feel like to go back to being young again without the memories I have now of my life and my children, because at the age of twenty-five they were not born. I won't remember Mimi because she came into my life quite late. I never would have dreamt, as a young person, of having a dragon as a mentor, spiritual guide and friend. Inside, a wave of panic surges – I am afraid of losing my beautiful golden dragon but then I hear her voice inside my head and I involuntarily pass into a receptive state to meet her as she greets me with a stoic stare, declaring:

"Now what's all this nonsense? Don't be such a baby! You know our connection, once made, can never be severed, so stop panicking! You have been given a great undertaking worthy of your abilities and you must do your best! I will always be here by your side and when you return we will resume our adventures together."

I smile, reassured by her words and feel the greatness of her love. I recall a time when I was very ill and see the scene in my mind as Mimi gently picks me up in her mouth. I was too ill to stand and she lays me softly on the tip of her warm tongue. Her sharp, jagged teeth never came close as she was so careful not to hurt me and together we flew across dark mountain ridges out towards an orange sun where purple shadows danced in a cobalt forest. At the edge of a verdant green lake she placed me where the healing water bubbled over white stones and sparkling spring water washed my body with restorative energy, revitalising every cell. Then she carried me to the edge of the forest and positioned me under the canopy of a lilac Cedar-tree, where the echo of tears whistled through the branches and fell like tender raindrops into my mouth. Drinking the sweet, magical elixir I grew better and stronger and was able to climb onto Mimi's back once more, to return home. Mimi smiles at my memory.

"Dragon law and draconian power, whether you remember it or not, will be in your subconscious mind and will help you in your quest. Remember, what you do for love attracts love, as like attracts like. Most of all, love yourself and the rest will follow."

I nod, swallowing back the tears, as I don't want to lose her or the memory of my children. Mimi sighs, knowing what I'm thinking and lets out an involuntary puff of steam uttering:

"Look my dear, you would be wise to adopt a little dragon law when coming to terms with parenthood. You understand in dragon law we birth, we nurture, we prepare and then let go! Humans must learn to do the same because every age and every stage of human life has a purpose, has a reason and on reaching the soul's winter, it is time to go back to the beginning and find that which has been lost along the pathway of life- to find the true self, the purpose of 'being'."

I move to throw my arms around her but she disappears leaving me with a warm sense of belonging.

Suddenly the video is interrupted by a waving Colonel apologising for not being present the next day for my regeneration process - he has a pressing engagement, but he concludes cheerfully with:

"Lots of luck for tomorrow, Soldier and remember that when you wake up you'll be fitter and stronger just like you were before!"

His image fades from the screen and I turn off the video having watched what I needed to see. I salute the empty screen declaring: "Thanks Colonel, no need to wish me luck, for I am Lucky."

XIAN ZU TRAINING

The sun is bright or is it a dazzling light shining in my eyes?

"Yes, she's awake now." A distant voice says. "Yes, all seems fine. Heart, lungs all majors clear. Process successfully executed. Give her time to come around and then proceed with the usual routine nurse. Let me know if anything amiss occurs," the doctor orders.

Silence descends and enfolds me as I slip back into a dream world. Do I feel different? I don't have time to answer my own question as darkness engulfs me in nothingness.

"That's right, sit up slowly. You might feel a little dizzy at first but that will soon pass," says a gentle nurse. She helps me sit up and I note how light my body feels. My arms are slender and my hands are smooth. Where is the wrinkled, veined skin of a senior citizen? I stare at my legs – dancer's legs and I shake my feet, feeling whole toes wriggling instead of stubs of double broken bones protruding on a disfigured foot. To dance is to sacrifice a normal existence where to push your body daily through physical pain becomes the norm. You learn to push through the pain barrier and dance through performances with broken toes. Dancing is a calling that a true performer cannot ignore. Only years later, when hips are worn to the bone, arthritic legs ache and bunioned feet cannot climb stairs, do you suffer the consequences of a lifetime of dance. Now aged twenty-five years, I can once again swing my legs freely over the bed and enjoy my lithe, athletic body gliding across the floor to the mirror. Is that really me? Tiny me with long flowing hair down to my waist? The Nurse laughs gleefully as she watches me pirouette across the room, delighting in my new-found body. Just as I dare myself to leap across the mat, the door opens and Doctor Zoburg enters uttering:

"I see we are awake and rearing to go!"

I smile and gently sit back on the side of the bed.

"What are the test results nurse?"

"All good doctor," replies the nurse, handing him a file to peruse.

"Ok. This afternoon you begin your physicals. You should be fine as you are in good shape, unlike last time!" affirms the Doctor. I nod, ready to meet the challenge but don't understand what he means by 'last time'. I have no recollection of a 'last time.'

"Everything will be provided for you and your strict regime must be adhered to if you are to be successful in your mission. Mr Alexander, Head of Assignment Training, will see you shortly to explain everything," she states officiously, bustling out of the door with her folders under her arm.

I know I am about to undertake an important mission and I have read the notes about being prepared to travel forward to bring back a little girl to our present time, but other details are vague and I am eager to learn more. A timid knock at my door disrupts my thoughts and I open it to find a small middle-aged man with a pale face and dark round glasses smiling a welcome. As he enters my room I note his clothes generally seem too large for him, like a little boy dressed in an adult suit. His comb-over black hair plastered to one side of his head, gives him a comic appearance. His arms are too long and his hands in which he carries a selection of pink folders, are too large for his small body. In his quiet non-assuming voice he says:

"I believe you have been expecting me? I'm Mr Alexander." He places the files on the table and holds out a wide, hairy hand which I shake.

"Shall we sit? We have a lot to discuss," he adds, calmly.

I am surprised that such a diminutive man, so polite, genteel and quiet holds such an important position. I was expecting a commanding, domineering man like the Colonel.

"I am here in my capacity as Head of Operations and as such will prepare you for your forthcoming mission. Please feel free to ask me any questions as and when they might arise," he assures in his soft, genteel voice and wide grin revealing large white teeth. I nod, gazing into his sombre brown eyes. He reminds me so much of a chimpanzee with his wide forehead, squat nose and thick rubbery lips. My Grandmother loves monkeys and even though she is in a home for the elderly, she still dances around and collects pictures of chimpanzees. I am lucky she is still alive as she says she is waiting to see great grandchildren before she pops her clogs! I think she will have to wait a long time as I have no intention of having children. A nurse intrudes with a hand-written message for Mr Alexander who politely apologises for the interruption and promises to return shortly.

"He is really sweet," I laugh, smiling at the nurse, "he reminds me so much of a monkey!"

The nurse shoots me a serious glance declaring," Mr Alexander is a highly acclaimed hybrid of human and chimpanzee and is extremely clever. We all greatly admire him and so please show him some respect!"

I am shocked and stop myself from laughing, thinking that explains his hands and posture and ill-fitting clothes. "I am sorry, I didn't mean to be disrespectful, it's just that he is so gentle."

"You don't know him!" retorts the nurse, "his calm exterior can change at any moment and then you will see how vicious he can be when his top lip rises bearing his sharp primate teeth. You won't think him gentle or sweet then! In his position, he is required to lead with disciplined authority."

I am silent and try to imagine the wrath of a monkey-man who seems so demur and polite," but how come he has such a powerful position?" I ask.

The nurse shrugging her shoulders says, "The hybrids are said to be super intelligent with superior physical traits, so I am sure that's why he's at the top."

I allow myself a little private joke imagining Mr Alexander with his super intellect swinging from light to light on the ceiling down the corridor, but as he swoops in through the door smiling, eager to return to our conversation, I don a serious face.

"Now to business Miss. We have a lot to get through in a short space of time as you are due to leave in one week."

I gasp. I had imagined I would be given longer to prepare for the mission.

"First things first," he says authoritatively, opening a pink file.

I find it hard to concentrate, my immature sense of humour still wants to wander down the path where Mr Alexander is swinging through trees and I have to hold myself in check.

"The outcome of your regeneration operation has been successful and you are now a fit, young lady of twenty-five years of age."

Mentally I add – 'with a mischievous sense of humour!' I had forgotten how the young have the insensibility to make fun of everything.

"Your training programme begins this afternoon and you will be following a Xian Zu agenda, taught by a Xian Zu Master, who will explain the philosophy behind the structure, but suffice it to know that Xian Zu is an ancient Chinese practice sought after by world leaders, Commanders, Spies and anyone who is in a position of authority. It requires, mind, body and soul training at the highest degree."

He shows me a short clip of people achieving the most impossible tasks such as catching flies with their hands, jumping across roof-tops, running barefoot over water, shooting arrows around corners and firing a gun to hit an unseen moving target and many other extraordinary feats.

"I don't think I will be able to do these things," I mutter.

"Ah, Miss, that's where you're wrong. First train the mind and the body will follow. You see small hinges can support enormous doors! You must remember...Desire...is your initial driving force because you must have the passion to want to achieve and be successful. Then you must 'Believe' because if you don't believe in yourself no one else will. Desire + Belief = CHANGE," he declares emphatically, "and believe me you will change!" He proclaims in a quiet, forceful voice. I suddenly glimpse a different Mr Alexander. A no-nonsense Mr Alexander who always gets his own way.

"Is that understood Miss?"

"Oh yes, yes," I affirm meekly.

"You will join the Xian Zu leadership course already in progress," he informs, eyeing me carefully over his large-rimmed glasses.

"Leadership?" I enquire puzzled, "I thought I was just going to get fit for the mission?"

"Indeed. Your father, during the Second World War became a hero and saved many men's lives, his fiery, Celtic temperament gave him courage. You have the same aptitude, but you do not know it yet."

Suddenly he leaps across the table and sweeps me up in his long primate arms and tucks me under his armpit, whilst jumping from one light fixture to the next to the open window where he dangles me out in mid-air. I am terrified. The drop below is nauseating. My eyes meet his. He is standing confidently on a tiny ledge outside the window while my legs are airborne. His eyes smile while mine are tearful. My whole body is shaking, my heart is thumping so hard I think it will break out of my chest! "There little Miss. Gently does it," he croons as he places me carefully next to him on the thin shelf. My legs are quivering and I desperately cling to his arm, afraid to let go in case I plunge to my death. "You have two choices-succeed or fail. Simple," he calmly adjusts his tie.

I am well aware of that. I can live or die and I don't need him to tell me that. He uncurls my fingers slowly from his jacket leaving me totally unsupported and stranded on the ledge. I push my back as far into the wall as I can, feeling the sharp pain of the bricks digging into my spine. The wind whistles across my face and my hair blows over my eyes. I daren't lift my hand to move it. A thought crosses my mind, as a cold feeling of emptiness engulfs me and I think I might just as well jump and end it all. It would be much easier, but I push that thought far away and tell myself I have to survive. I try to inch my way back to the window, but I am paralysed. My feet and my legs are stuck to the ledge.

Suddenly Mr Alexander leaps out into the air. I close my eyes. The shock hits the pit of my stomach and sick rises in my throat causing a burning sensation but I swallow it back. Something touches my feet and I open my eyes. Mr Alexander is smiling up at me, his hands resting on the ledge. He lets go with one hand and swings out laughing then glides back in again with both hands touching my feet.

"Come on, one foot after the other. Baby steps to reach the window. The Universe loves baby steps and will always reward small efforts, diligently offered."

I feel his hand lift my foot and I allow him to guide me carefully to the window to safety. I don't know how I got back to my seat but I sit staring at him from across the desk as though nothing has happened and I am left wondering if I just imagined the whole episode.

"Yes, back to leadership," he declares nonchalantly," and what do you think the qualities of a good leader are?"

I am still puzzled by what I think just happened and I can't answer.

"Well, it requires a firm base. That means you have to be confident in your own abilities and your judgement. It requires a strong hand, you must be able to carry out your decisions alone, swiftly and without hesitation. You need a kind mouth and a deep understanding of what is fair and finally, you must have clear eyes to see all."

I listen to his wise words and bow to his authority. I have much to learn.

"Xian Zu will teach you all. You are shaking?"

I nod, feeling oddly out of synchronisation with the world.

"You are in shock because you cannot believe what has just happened."

"I am just relieved to know that it did happen and that it wasn't just my imagination!" I tell him.

"You are stuck in your routine world and if you are to discover who you really are, you must adapt to new and unfamiliar ideas by opening up your imagination, because that's where you really exist. But the trick is to be in both the outer world and inner at the same time. Blending the two makes you strong and gives you an advantage over others who have no insight."

I sigh, hearing his words but understanding and putting into practice the philosophy is hard. I am afraid of the unknown. Afraid that I will fail. I am fearful of everything.

"I know you're afraid and that is very natural for someone in your position but your training will help you overcome all. Keep in mind this little rhyme:

'When bleak is the home of your comfort zone,

When emptiness is your friend,

When fear rides by your side

Speak out and change the tide."

He laughs jovially at his little rhyme slapping his thighs and clapping his hands like a circus monkey.

"Speak out and change the tide, don't you think that's great?" he continues laughing. I find it hard to laugh but manage to smile a little. I feel like someone has hacked into the 'confidence' file in my mind.

"So there we are dear. All set for your new adventure. Enjoy the Xian Zu experience and I will see you again soon," he bows as he exits and I am left alone to ponder the dreaded training. My thoughts are interrupted by an assistant who brings a light lunch served on a white tray and also places a white uniform, consisting of baggy trousers and a Chinese-style top, on the bed.

"Please wear these for your training. An assistant will take you over to the gym shortly," the young girl says. I thank her and peck at the bean salad. I am not hungry. I dress in the uniform and check the mirror. I look like a martial arts student and with my hair tied back I am ready to 'change the tide!'

I am taken to an old-fashioned gym with wooden ladders and ropes dangling from the ceiling. The floor consists of roughly polished wooden blocks that have clearly seen a great deal of action. Waiting in the centre is a group of nine students all dressed in white Xian Zu uniforms. They are standing at ease in a circle with a woman instructor planted in the middle. As I enter she calls:

"Ah here is our tenth student everyone. Now we have five boys and five girls. Tell us your name."

"Lucky!" I reply shyly.

"I see, LOW KEY."

I want to correct her but she declares: "Madam. You address me as Madam. Women Masters are called Madam. Men Masters are called Master. Is that clear LOW KEY?" Her voice rises to a crescendo, echoing around the high ceiling.

I nod, intimidated by her challenging attitude. I desperately want to correct her and tell her my name is Lucky, but I dare not!

"You, you that is you and all of you," she points like an angry Sergeant Major at all of us, "are Space Cadet students and will be addressed as 'Cadet'. Understood?"

We all reply in unison, "Yes, Madam."

"Xian Zu means – does anyone know?" She asks as she parades around the outer circle of our group. No one replies.

"I see, well Xian means high spiritual, supreme, high-powered and ZU means to organise, so the training helps to mould you into a superior being, but it is your responsibility to organise your development yourself. That means ultimately you are in charge of your own destiny. Oh sweet ones,"

"Xian Zu has many layers to its teaching, one of which shows you how to gain the most sensuous pleasure from eating food; for example, you are instructed on which area the of mouth you should eat certain foods to derive the most sensuous pleasure and how to drink certain drinks as well as what drinks you should imbibe for the specific nutrients they contain. Perhaps one day you might be fortunate enough to attend a Xian Zu banquet are you eager to do that? Let us continue. Your training involves MIND-BODY-SPIRIT harmony. Harmony like singing," she sings at the top of her voice 'lah' and holds the note for a long time, putting everyone on edge. I don't know whether to laugh or cry, but I guess her purpose is to disorientate us all and she is succeeding!

"Is that a smile I detect Cadet?" She points at a shy male, peering closely into his eyes." Well answer me boy!" She screams.

"Yes, I mean, no, I mean I don't know!" He blurts out nervously.

"Smile, laugh, cry, I don't mind. Do whatever you please," she states miming each emotion as though she is performing on stage to a large audience. "All is emotion. Emotion is vibration. Vibration is frequency that can be picked up by the enemy. Laugh... I said laugh all of you!"

We look at each other and feign laughter.

"Louder! Louder!" our instructor shrieks and we respond. There you see, the air is filled with sound resonance and it carries far. "Now cry. Go on cry!" She demands, flailing her arms in the air as though conducting an orchestra. We attempt sham crying and she dances around the room as though in a trance. Then she suddenly leaps into the centre of the circle and shouts, "Stop!" and we all immediately respond and stand to attention. Is she crazy I wonder? Yet somehow, there is something about her technique I recognise.

"Ah, there, there," she mockingly murmurs, patting a boy on the head, "crying is a different emotion. A different vibration and can travel through walls, can it not Cadets?"

"Yes Madam," we affirm in unison.

"Now my loves, my little turtle doves, answer me this question. Your life depends on it- tell me what brought you here today?"

The first boy shrugs his shoulders and replies, "I brought myself."

"You stupid, stupid boy! Sit down – you are dead!" She screams in his face.

A girl nudges forward and answers, "My desire to learn."

Madam's face puckers in disgust and she pushes the girl down on the floor shouting, "You are too clever!" Another boy dares a reply saying, "a taxi brought me here!" At which Madam flies into a terrible rage and throws the boy on the floor. Each Cadet in turn offers an answer which she rejects forcefully and each student is knocked to the floor until she reaches me and stands menacingly in front of me with a sarcastic smile, and in a mocking tone asks:

"And you my dear LOW KEY, what brought you here today?"

I feel I have to state the obvious as all other answers have failed and I reply meekly, "My feet, my feet brought me here!"

At first, Madam grimaces with anger and then a smile creases her cheeks and derisively but softly she says, "Yes, of course, my dear. Your feet brought you here. Is she the only one with any intelligence, you imbeciles?" She glares at the rest of the group.

The others sigh, realising that they too should have stated the obvious.

"You see my dears, my little cherubs, my petlings, the most obvious choice is often the hardest to recognise. You have heard of phrases like- 'can't see the wood for the trees' and 'hidden in plain sight' which describe confusing situations designed to send you in the wrong direction. Before you try to fathom intricate clues, look for the obvious. Now because of your stupidity, you are all dead, except for this worthy Cadet. Stand here my sweet one, next to me."

I follow her orders, nervously. I don't trust her and feel awkward as the others stand shame-faced, having failed the first test.

"Now my loved ones, stand in a circle, come on wider, you will answer my questions. The first Cadet to reach the centre of the circle is the winner. Now listen carefully. What colour is sky-blue-pink with the colour washed out?" All the cadets look puzzled, one answers 'pink' another 'blue' another 'purple'. I raise my hand and Madam nods for me to respond and I answer- 'there is no colour!"

"Little Miss Clever clogs has the right answer. Tell them! Explain!" She shouts with disdain.

"Well you said, the colour is washed out, so there is no colour," I reply timidly.

"She is right, of course! Words, words my dears, listen to them. I know how to make them disappear in a sentence, I can disguise them by the way I use them while still getting the meaning across. I can suggest things and place them in your subconscious to influence you. Do not underestimate the power of auto-suggestion. Remember 'in plain sight'?"

"Ah, I should have known." one girl sighs.

"You should have listened. You should have analysed. You should use your common sense. You should question," Madam stamps, pounding the floor with her feet.

"Now we will play a little game, my darlings," she laughs in a high-pitched trill," a game my loves where you have to listen, think and then act. I want two teams in two lines facing me. Join together like a choo-choo train. Yes, my loves we are going to play trains." She squawks at the group and then turns to me whispering, "Not you, you sit down."

Her face changes as she looks at me and I wonder what game she is playing with me. I have to admit the tests seem familiar and I do know the answers. Maybe I have a faint recollection from my life in the future, but if I do, it's cloudy. I know the game of 'trains' from somewhere, but I can't remember from where. I watch as Madam leads them into a trap.

"You are two trains in a station waiting to go. When I give the order you will move. Understand?"

"Yes Madam," chorus the Cadets.

"The train now standing on platform four is the four sixty-two going to Edinburgh. Go!" She shouts enthusiastically as they all take off shunting like children in the playground.

Madam shouts "Dead! Dead! Dead! You're all dead! Lie down! Think! THIINK!" Why are you dead? Why are you all dead Cadet?" She shouts pointing at a quaking boy who has no idea what he has done wrong. I know the answer and watch as the other poor students are brow-beaten and hounded by Madam who shouts:

"Because, you stupid idiots, there is no such time as four sixty-two. There can be no time at all with sixty-two minutes in the hour. How many minutes in the hour?"

"Sixty Madam!" They all shout.

"Oh, I mustn't get flustered- must I?" she asks her invisible self. She moves to become her invisible self and replies in a high-pitched voice, "No, don't get flustered, be nice to the dearlings!" She gazes sweetly at her invisible self and returns to the students who don't know whether to laugh or cry. Then Madam prances around the room pretending to ride a horse, brushes invisible dust off her shoulders and returns to her commanding self, stating calmly,

"We will now try again. You see I lead you all into a trap simply because you did not listen to the words. If you were in charge of a platoon of soldiers and you misread or misunderstood instructions, everyone could be dead because of your incompetence. Now we will try again. Get into two trains. Listen to the instruction -'the train now standing on platform two is the cancelled three thirty-four travelling to London and is now ready to board. GO!"

I watch the students move indecisively. Some stand still but overall they all move to the 'go' command. Now Madam freaks out in a temper tantrum unlike anything we have witnessed before. She beats each Cadet to the ground and jumps up and down flaying them with the foulest language, making each one feel stupid and inadequate.

"Tell them, tell them LOW KEY!" She is out of breath, almost collapsing.

I stand up and say apologetically: "you can't board a train that's been cancelled. It's not there!"

"Precisely my little puddings, oh chiffly ones, hey diddlely dee, come with me, we'll try again. Stand up! Stand up!" she sings gaily. "Now the train standing on platform seven is the delayed midday train travelling to Peterborough boarding through gate nine...GO!"

Some students go while a few others stand still. Madam pushes those standing to the ground and those moving she strokes gently on the shoulder calling them 'loves'.

"You, Cadet Number two," Madam points at me "tell them why you were able to go!"

"Because the train is only delayed, which means that it can still go. Delayed does not mean cancelled."

"Oh you joy of joys, you pretty one. My heart's delight you are right," sings Madam. "Now you are getting it! Words are weighty and can be manipulated to lead you astray. If you are undercover on a mission you could betray your disguise to the enemy just by missing a minor detail. You must pay close attention to specifics. It could make the difference between life and death."

I understand the training. It is so familiar to me, almost like second nature. Madam makes her way over to me and whispers: "keep it low key." I am not sure what she means. Is she telling me to keep a low profile because I know the answers? I thought she was being clever by pretending to mispronounce my name, but perhaps she wasn't. Do I have Xian Zu knowledge from the future? My mind is blank as Madam prepares to play another 'mind' game.

"It seems to me you are all so brain-washed into responding to words that are 'commands' such as 'stop' 'go' 'backwards' 'forwards' that you jump automatically to the directives. This game is where you must respond immediately to the command but all the orders are opposite. So Cadets up means down and down means up. Stop means go and go means stop. Backwards means forwards and forwards means backwards. Slow means fast and fast means slow."

I watch as the Cadets fall over themselves confused by the opposing commands and I understand what Madam is trying to achieve in retraining the mind to respond quickly to words embedded in the brain interpreting their meaning to adapt promptly to a new set of rules. This training is invaluable to leaders, commanders, spies and undercover agents, teaching them to be adaptable and to use their brain and mind power more effectively.

"Now my loves, my turtle doves, you have made a complete mess of that exercise. You see how you are all brain-washed into obeying commands without thinking for yourself. Now you will all pour yourselves a glass of water and watch it flow into the glass. Do not drink it, watch it. What do you see?"

"Nothing...it's just water," laughs a boy.

Madam immediately strides over to him, snatches the glass out of his hand and throws the water in his face. The class laughs and she scolds them yelling, "This is not a laughing matter! You stupid boy, sit over there, I don't want to see your face!"

The class is suddenly serious and quiet.

"Well, the rest of you, what do you see?"

"A clear liquid," a girl pipes up, looking deeply into the glass.

"Yes and how does a liquid move?" Madam probes quietly.

The students shake their heads afraid to give the wrong answer – in case she pours water over them.

"Well I'll tell you, I'll show you," she sings dancing, gliding and swaying as she croons, "Water glides, it flows, it's fluid, it ripples, it rears up, it drips, it meanders…. Get the picture?"

"Yes Madam," reply the Cadets in a monotone drone.

"Water takes the path of least resistance. You should be like water. Water will slip underground when it needs to but will always find a way back to the surface. Water has many faces and many shades. It can be still or softly muscular; it can roar like a lion and as much as it can be life-sustaining it can kill in an instant. When it meets fire it transcends into steam and disappears into the ether. You must learn to pour water into your spirit and let life flow. You can learn much from this wonderful element."

There is silence as she lulls everyone into a false sense of security through her hypnotic trickery. Suddenly she bellows at the top of her voice 'BOOM!' and the class jump and spill their water over themselves in shock. Madam laughs screeching, "You were not vigilant. You could have been killed! I could have been a tsunami. I could have been an avalanche. I could have been a raging river, I could have been a storm and you my dear babies, were asleep. Now you are all dead!"

The afternoon wears on, the mind-control awareness instruction continues and at one point Madam gives me a few cadets to instruct in vocal training and how to use the voice effectively to hypnotise, mislead and misguide people. She knows I know how. I am pleased she trusts me to carry out the instruction. I explain to the students that everyone has three ranges to their voice -high, medium and low.

I show them how to access and use each register, describing how each sound has a particular vibration and can be effectively used to achieve certain goals. I demonstrate seductive, persuasive, breathy sounds from the chest which can be used to lure people into traps. I show them how their normal voice, fluctuating through all three registers is more effective than a monotone medium sound and can help people to remember information more efficiently. Also, I tell them, the 'head register' – a high-pitched tone can stop people or give an effective warning signal in an emergency.

When everyone has gone and the gym heaves an empty sigh of relief, I watch Madam return to her true self. She is an actress and trained in the art of performance. In reality, she is a gentle, kind person, rather shy and now she slides discreetly and inconspicuously out of the door, unrecognisable in her drab clothes, blending into the crowd. I have been told that the most successful spies are those who merge unnoticeably into the congregation and Madam does this with ease.

The week passes quickly in a round of physical training and learning how to overcome physical and mental obstacles. True Xian Zu methods of handling strange, unforeseen situations are instilled into the brain and instincts are honed, sharpened and polished to the highest degree. By the end of the training, I feel confident to tackle the mission and I am called to Mr Alexander's office where Madam sits demurely by the window.

"Ah come in Cadet," hails Mr Alexander, holding out a large hairy hand for me to shake. "I understand the training has gone well and you are now ready to tackle the assignment?"

I nod in agreement, suddenly catching a fly in mid-air. Mr Alexander smiles knowingly and says, "Well now, you will be taken tomorrow to the portal where you will be teleported to the future.

"Portal?"

Mr Alexander laughs, "Why, yes! Portals to other universes, other time zones, other spheres have existed forever. Doorways to the beyond play an important part in all forms of life, everywhere. When

Moses parted the Dead Sea, it was through a portal. How do you think the legendary Merlin could appear and disappear in Arthurian times? It was because of his knowledge of portals. How do you think Pythagoras, Leonardo da Vinci, Einstein, Nikola Tesla gained their special knowledge? It was through portal travel to the beyond. Did you know that Earth is a stop-off station for extra-terrestrials because the planet is close to a portal to another universe? My dear, there is a hotel in Washington that was built around a portal and from the outside looks ordinary, but inside on the fourth floor is a special elevator that is a time machine and transports people and beings to other spheres." I gasp. I have no knowledge of portals and yet the information seems credible.

"You will be met by our agent Marillion who will take you under her wing and help you in your mission to retrieve the little girl and bring her back to this time zone."

"That's fine! I am sure I will be able to do that," I reply confidently.

"Yes, I'm sure, but it may not be as straightforward as you think," Madam says quietly.

Mr Alexander coughs and shuffles in his chair affirming Madam's statement, adding, "Yes, you see my dear, we are not the only ones wishing to, let us put it this way, wishing to save Marta. Others want to abduct her to groom her for the Presidency. That is to say, to train her in evil ways for their own greedy, selfish profit. You see we cannot change the future-it is assured that she will be America's first black woman President, but we can make sure that her childhood is protected in a good, loving family, so that she is brought up with fair family values, a good education and a solid grounding for leadership. That is where you come in. You must make sure, for the sake of our future, that she is brought back to us, so that we can nurture her through the 'goodness' channel."

"That's a tall order. Are you saying that if I don't bring her back, there will be an evil woman in the President's chair?" I ask.

"Quite simply, yes," Mr Alexander says, his tone serious. Suddenly the 3D screen on the back wall flickers and the Colonel greets us all cheerily, expressing his best wishes for my mission and congratulating me on completing the training successfully.

"Mr Alexander is she fully informed?" enquires the Colonel.

"Well, Sir, we are just in the process of explaining everything."

"You see Soldier, it's a little more complicated and involved than we anticipated. But don't worry, you've got a great back-up team waiting to help you and I know you will succeed. You won't let me down. That's all for now, bon voyage."

The Colonel's final words fade as his image clouds and Mr Alexander refers to his notes. "Early in the morning you will be taken to a secret location where the portal will be activated and you will slip easily into the future" he says.

"Is it dangerous?" I enquire nervously.

"Not at all my dear, it's been tried and tested for thousands of years."

"Then why are dangerous time machines used in the future?"

"Greed, my dear, sheer greed. Men made time machines to imitate the portals to gain wealth. The machines, unless government-engineered, are not a hundred percent safe, but the portals are - believe me."

I nod and am satisfied with his explanation. Madam assures me that all will be well and smiles.

"Can I ask you a question?" I ask.

"Of course," she answers.

"How did I know the answers to the Xian Zu mind training?"

"That's easy," she grins," in the future, you are a Grand Xian Zu Master Teacher. You have no recollection of it now, but your memory cells will still be active in certain areas. That's how you knew the answers. That's why I needed you to keep quiet and be low key."

I understand everything and feel relieved to know that in the future I will develop a greater spiritual awareness.

"Now Lucky, I wish you every success and maybe we will meet again. Remember that 'good intention brings good results and the

best intention creates life out of a dead space! Go in love Lucky"
beams Madam.

She called me Lucky, she said my name correctly, for the first
time. She said 'Lucky' for indeed I am and will be!

FORWARDS, BACKWARDS TO THE PRESENT

It is the morning of the big day and I am woken early by an assistant and taken to the lobby where a man in a black uniform escorts me to a large, black limousine. It is dark outside and the centre is empty. I am not sad to be leaving, I have completed my training and I am ready for the next challenge.

"Would you like some music Miss?" asks the driver, "I find it helps pass the time. We've got a long way to go."

I agree with his suggestion, especially as the windows are blacked out and I can't see anything outside. The driver's choice of music is not mine but I don't complain as he seems pleasant and I don't want to disturb his concentration. I fall asleep a few times before we finally stop and then the driver disappears. A large man with a bald head opens the door and pops inside the car stating:

"Hello Miss, I'm Bill. I've come to accompany you to your destination. Please put this on and take my arm. I will guide you." His accent is familiar reminding me of hot days and holidays on a far-off island, but I can't quite remember where. Bill's thick-set body is like a boxer built for strength and he is dressed in a black suit, like a body-guard. I obey him without question as he places a thick, black mask over my eyes and I take his strong arm to support myself. He gently assists me out of the car, planting my feet firmly on the ground before we move. I sense it is still light although I have no idea of the time, except that my empty stomach is complaining.

"Now we are going to walk forward. Don't worry, I've got you!" he says reassuringly.

He is good at his job and I wonder how many victims he has led to their final destination, but I dispel empty, negative thoughts and promise myself only to think positively, as I have been taught, even although blind man's bluff was not one of my favourite games as a child because I hated the visionless sensation. Now I have no choice but to be led somewhere by a total stranger.

"Not far now Miss, just a few more paces. You're doing fine."

I don't feel fine, in fact I want to be sick.

"That's it-step inside Miss. Nearly there," he declares.

I guess we are inside a lift as I hear him press a button and there is a sensation of gliding upwards. When the lift stops he gently shunts me out into a cold corridor. I glean it's a corridor of some kind as our footsteps echo as we walk. When we stop I hear him open a door, then he takes off my blindfold and I blink as my eyes adjust to the light. After a few seconds, I see a plush-red suite and the familiar man seated behind a large oak desk, who smiles a welcome.

"Here she is Mr President, safe and sound," announces Bill.

"Welcome my dear. Please take a seat."

I am not sure how to address him or what to do, so I quickly sit down at the desk.

"You know you have a very important task ahead young lady and I want to thank you in person before you leave."

"Thank you Sir, thank you," I blurt out, a little embarrassed.

"We will do our best on our part to make sure you are well supported on every level. Help will not be too far away at any given time, so don't be afraid. Now you will be prepared for your trip and remember leaders always accomplish what they set out to do!" He shakes my hand as I am led away by an attractive young woman to another suite where clothes are laid out on a large double bed. Black denim jeans, black hard-core boots, a black sweatshirt and a black leather jacket in my size have been prepared for my journey. When I am dressed, the young woman places a black cap on my head and the ensemble is complete. I look like a heroine in a fast action thriller movie. The woman takes me to a set of double doors where she places her hands over a screen and a gadget drops down to take her iris print. Next her whole body is scanned and a skeletal X ray appears on a screen opposite. Another set of doors open and we walk into a large arena where people in white coats are busy adjusting dials and testing apparatus. At the far end of the dark arena is a pulsing circle of purple, red and blue, revolving, hypnotic lights. At first the mesmerising beams appear on the surface of a round door but as I get closer, I can see that they are part of a long tunnel boring deep inside a channel, undulating far into the distance. A man in a black uniform approaches and takes my arm explaining,

"You just walk gently inside the tunnel. There is nothing to be afraid of."

Now as I near the entrance, the powerful electronic beams pull me forwards and I am afraid. I hadn't expected the overwhelming, intense force to be so fearsome. I don't want to go inside. The pressure pulling me in is terrifying. My instincts tell me that if I step inside I will be incinerated and burnt to a cinder. I shake my head and walk backwards. I need to sit down. No one prepared me for this. It is too much! Someone brings me a seat and the man in the black uniform pats my shoulder. "Look I know how you feel. It's tremendously overpowering the first time you see the portal and feel its powerful energy, but honestly it's fine once you walk inside!"

"I'll be burnt alive!" I cry.

The man gently laughs and nods his head saying," well in a manner of speaking, yes, that's what happens. All the cells in your body are transported and re-aligned in a different time zone. But you won't feel a thing. Believe me!"

I shake my head. The vastness, the intensity, the breath-taking density are too much. It's like standing on the edge of a bubbling volcano where the scorching heat from bubbling lava burns my face.

"Look I tell you what, our Commander is scheduled to travel just after you. We could ask him to go first and you can watch him enter. We can talk to him on the other side when he arrives so that you can be reassured that all is well."

I don't reply. I am deeply shocked by the mighty ferociousness and potency of the electrical waves reaching out of the portal. I feel its tentacles sucking me in and I don't want to go near it.

"Our Commander says it's ok and he'll go first. Watch him, it's easy!"

I turn towards the hypnotic glare and watch the tall Commander, dressed in army combat gear approach the portal. His black silhouette outlined against the bright flames, he stands firm as the inferno engulfs his body. At first the purple red and blue flashes bounce off his frame, blazing in a quirky flamenco dance as he proceeds farther into the tunnel, then the rays seep into his body like blotting paper soaking up ink, until only a shadow remains which twitches for a few seconds and then disappears in the dying flames. In the silence a voice echoes from a speaker:

"All clear. Target reached. Tell her I'm OK." The voice breaks off and the officer in black helps me to stand, saying calmly:

"There you are you see. There's nothing to it. Come on it's your turn."

He takes my arm firmly and I am lead, like a sacrificial lamb, quaking with fear as I approach the hungry flames. I am terrified to be consumed by the fire. I stop at the edge of the portal. I cannot enter. I refuse. Then, a mighty push from behind hurls me forwards into the fire. The flames leap around me but to my surprise and delight they are neither hot nor cold. It is like taking a warm shower. There is a light buzzing in my ears and I look down to see my feet disappearing, then my torso disintegrates and finally all of me is consumed. There is no pain, no feeling, only elation! Somewhere beyond, my body reconstructs and I re-form and find myself standing in a dim light. I look down at my bare feet and my naked body. I blink as I hear lewd male laughter echo around the room. Horrible dirty faces glare as I am scrutinised by grotesque monsters. A man leers and laughs reaching out with his greasy hands to touch me. I scream, trying to cover my body to protect myself. Suddenly, from the crowd, four men and a woman spring into action slashing out mercilessly, carving everyone to pieces in a butchered blood bath, with their laser rays.

The woman turns me away from the massacre and cloaks me in a blanket whipping me away to a waiting flying capsule, which glides seamlessly into the busy sky. As I sit next to her in the tiny capsule my body shakes involuntarily and my teeth chatter. No one explained that my clothes would disintegrate in the tunnel and that I might be off-target on my re-entrance.

"Don't worry, your body will soon adjust to the new frequency. The shaking will soon stop. It's just a reaction to the process," she states calmly. "By the way, I'm Marillion, call me Mari."

"What the hell happened back there?" I demand.

"The rival faction, Corrival, know how to deflect the portal pathway and can easily redirect your destination to wherever they wish. We, on the other hand know exactly when they refract the pulse and with that information we can track where and when you will arrive. They know who you are and why you're here and they want to snatch Marta before we do and nothing will stop them trying."

I am silent trying to adjust to a new body in a different time zone, attempting to make sense of the information Mari is giving me. I watch her skilfully steer the vehicle through the skies dodging flying cars, small aircraft and strange-looking flying bicycles. She is about twenty years of age with a beautiful, sculpted Indian face and a lithe, athletic body. She is wearing camouflage army gear with her long hair tied up in a bun. Instinctively, I trust her. The air is buzzing with flying machines of all kinds. Some contraptions I have never seen before whiz past nearly scraping our door and I duck involuntarily as they zoom by.

"Hold on!" commands Mari, as she drives straight towards a tall building displaying current news on its façade. We dive head-on towards the centre of the screen and I close my eyes fearing the worst. I squint as we pass through the middle of a man's face on the screen and glide through the brickwork entering a dark garage lit dimly with side lights. Mari laughs at my shocked expression and taunts:

"Gotcha! I just love to see their faces every time! Great smoke-screen don't you think?"

I nod, recovering my breath.

"This is our headquarters. For the present, it's quite safe. Come on I'll show you around."

She leads the way through the car park where a handful of odd-looking vehicles are parked, then out through dark double doors into a long, carpeted corridor. Mari explains that their H.Q. is built on the inside cavity of an old theatre which has long been abandoned, so the shape follows the contour of the theatre in a large square. The corridor is narrow but the rooms leading off are quite substantial. "This is Head Office," she opens a door into a large functional room with personnel tracking 3D maps floating in mid- air and gadgets receiving information from drones as small as flies perched in secret places and communication booths where you can send a holographic image of yourself to anywhere in the world. There are 3D printing machines that can punch out guns or weapons and so much amazing new technology that my head spins in amazement.

"Come on, I'll show you the board room, where we will meet this evening. This is the common room and the kitchen. My room and yours is down the hall where you will keep Marta with you until you are scheduled to leave, which shouldn't be too long!" Mari says.

I peep inside my room, there are no windows because the complex is created inside the walls of the old theatre and as Mari explains their presence is harder to detect without windows, although, she tells me, there are devices which can see inside any enclosure. A new set of clothes is laid out ready for me on a small dresser and I quickly become one of Mari's colleagues dressed in a grey jump suite with a black belt. I feel ready and confident to tackle my mission and it seems they have thought of everything as the clothes are my size and look quite good, as far as combat gear goes!

"Come on let's go eat. I expect you're hungry now?" I hadn't thought about food but now the suggestion triggers a hunger pang and I follow her into the high-tech world of culinary wizardry where any food or drink can be conjured up at the touch of a button.

"We have a record of all your favourite food and drink which has already been posted into the system so, what is it to be?" Mari asks jovially. I am a little astonished and ask her to surprise me.

She nods and whirs into action, pressing buttons, shaking pots with pulsing lights, pouring glistening liquid into odd luminescent beakers and finally a tray full of my favourite seafood dishes appears from nowhere, with a bottle of champagne. We both laugh gleefully and she sets my meal out on a sliding table which appears miraculously out of the wall. I watch her as she quickly prepares herself an Indian meal accompanied by the best red wine. It's like dining in the finest restaurant without the fuss of other people around. A couple of young men pop in and remind us that we have a board meeting scheduled in half an hour, so we must not dally and need to finish our meal quickly and tidy up. Everything is placed into a steel machine where cups, food – waste, plates, cutlery – everything is sorted, cleaned, sifted, pulped and prepared ready for the next meal. There is a high-tech bathroom in my room with all the latest sanitary gadgets and hygienic apparatus, so I freshen up for the meeting and begin to feel more like myself again.

In the board room, which is a multi-media operations unit, we gather to discuss the recovery strategy for Marta. I sit slightly behind and to the side of Mari and notice a small electronic cell in the nape of her neck which beams an almost imperceptible light. I ask her about it and she says everyone in operations has a chip, linked to Head Office.

"We are, if you like, fully 'transhuman' that is to say that we have super-human intelligence and superior human physical prowess," she laughs, "it's quite normal, you know. Oh sorry I forgot, you are from the pre-transhumanism era."

I detect a hint of sympathy in her voice as though she feels sorry for me because I am not imbued with the latest technology. I watch fascinated as different species of Alien hybrids enter the room, each eyeing me scrupulously. Mari explains the different types of being as they bring their specialist skills to the table. All of them are far more intelligent than the human race.

"He is a Blue Avion," she explains as the tall bird bipod enters.

The being is a beautiful bird man. I love the iridescent colours on his head plume, ranging from electric blue, azure and baby blue through to pale blue, like a calm Mediterranean sea in the sunshine.

His face is bird-like with a beak similar to a duck's bill and his body is covered in tiny blue feathers. His eyes are dark as a blackbird's and he has two forefingers that are longer than the others. I am told he is a very spiritual being with a great sense of justice and fairness and his people live in the fifth density, travelling to earth to help humans.

Then a translucent being shimmers across the room. Her shape is female. She glistens like dewy raindrops in the early morning mist and Mari explains that she is an Arcturian, one of the highest spiritually aware beings that exist in the fifth dimension.

"The Arcturians are, in essence, pure love and light and are great healers. They are special guardians of children and they will not allow anyone near their young unless they have the colour purple in their aura," states Mari.

I love the colour purple and hope that the Arcturian approves of me and my quest to save Marta. Next to enter are Aliens who more closely resemble humans.

"They are tall whites," Mari points to three very tall beings who could quite easily be mistaken for Scandinavian humans. The two women are attractive and have long straggly white hair and beautiful pale skin. They look like Vogue models and the man is slightly taller also with long white hair and a handsome face. "The tall whites have been on earth for a long time," explains Mari," and they tend to live in remote places like deserts, but often mingle with ordinary people in cities and towns; they even go out for meals with their families. Their presence on earth deters other, more hostile Aliens, from attacking the planet, so they have a vested interest in the success of our mission."

Everyone is quiet as a V.I.P. enters. Mari whispers:

"He is the Chief. He is a class 5 Humanoid."

I can't ask her to explain further as the meeting begins but I can see that he is a large, thick-set being with a face that is almost human apart from the fact that it is distorted, with strange patterns imprinted on his forehead. He doesn't have hair and his well-built body is encased in a silver suit. He doesn't speak but communicates telepathically with everyone. I am surprised when I hear his voice in my head, it's like listening to a lecture on my headphones. He welcomes all gathered, especially myself and everyone turns to acknowledge me. I blush awkwardly and look away as he talks of the importance of the mission and how for the sake of peace and unity of planet earth, it is necessary to make sure Marta is brought up in a loving environment. He takes us to the compound through drone communication and we see her sleeping on a pile of rags in the corner of a crowded dormitory.

"She is unkempt, uncared for and frequently left to run wild. Most of the time she is starving and has very little interaction with the other children or adults. Those in charge are seen as merely keepers to feed and tame the motley zoo. Most children are abused by adults and some children abuse others, smaller than themselves. This is the pitiful state in which we will find Marta. Now I hand you over to Commander Troy who is in charge of operation Marta."

The Commander in a khaki uniform steps forward. He is a 'transhuman' and has a strong athletic body with a rugged face and kind eyes.

"This is the plan," he states as a 3D map rolls down from an invisible anchor. "The compound is heavily guarded, not because of precious cargo inside but because the government do not want to lose their cheap child labour. Also they sell children when they are old enough to undertake other work. Mari is going in as an undercover buyer, seeking to purchase suitable young girls for her establishment."

I am shocked that so far ahead in the future, this kind of trafficking still exists. My thought is answered instantly, in my head - 'you can't stamp out human nature so easily'. I see the Arcturian lady nod in my direction and I understand the message comes telepathically from her.

"Mari will be given the chance to view a few well-chosen girls and when she enters the compound she will send our little friend the ladybird here to seek out Marta. If you are not acquainted with this technology I will explain that our little friend can attach itself to the target in question and communicate, guide, act as a weapon and steer our target home. It can even lift a target clear of any obstruction in its wake. When attached, it can fly the target five feet above the ground for a short distance. Once it attaches itself to the target it will not let go until commanded to do so. Pretty neat isn't it?"

I nod, amazed at the gadget's ability as such a tiny object in the shape of a ladybird, to accomplish so much.

"Once our little friend here has attached itself to the target it will be at our command and we will be able to act as we see fit at the time. Meanwhile Mari will have purchased ten girls and will be allowed to take them to safety, saving them from a terrible life. The time allotted for the visit fits in with the nap time of the younger children and half-day change-over of staff, so there won't be many guards or keepers around."

The humanoid agrees to the plans and everyone else affirms the course of action.

"Excuse me Sir," I interject gingerly," what do I do?"

"Well, just wait until Marta is brought here and then your work will begin!" He chuckles.

"But I thought I was supposed to get her?" I question.

"Well, that plan is deemed to be too dangerous and we need a transhuman to tackle the job."

I fall silent, understanding and accepting the decision. I note that my question seems to have caused a bit of concern among the Aliens who ban together for a moment until the Arcturian stands up and addresses everyone:

"Our human friend should be allowed to accompany the mission," she asserts, calmly.

"As we discussed, that's not absolutely necessary. She might even be at risk," maintains Commander Troy.

The Blue Avion rises and insists that I accompany the operations team. The Commander backs down and agrees to let me go with Mari on the understanding that I don't take an active role in any duties. I agree. I am grateful to the Aliens for fighting my cause, although I don't quite understand their motive. The meeting draws to a close and the Arcturian lady glides over towards me. She is so beautiful and ethereal with her shimmering light body quivering gently.

"Be at peace my loved one. Love light and knowledge will steer you clear. You have visited our ship-is that not so?"

I nod remembering my remote viewing quest to visit an Arcturian ship where I was granted entrance to a most incredible world. It was a vast, humongous cigar-shaped ship. The outer core was made of indestructible brown metallic material and inside was a softer protective skin which shrank as I sailed inside. I was taken to the 'calming garden' by iridescent beings which was a glorious luscious meadow where visitors had their negative vibrations from the outside world, smoothed away, because Arcturians vibrate on a higher level to other beings and any form of negativity would be detrimental to them.

"You were allowed to visit our children, were you not?" She softly enquires.

"Yes, I was privileged to do so and we had a wonderful time. They thought I was very funny," I admit. She smiles sharing my recollection of being guided into a small dark room where little light beings sparkling with multi-coloured energy, sitting in a semi-circle with elder beings hovering behind them. They asked me to perch on the end of the row while they introduced themselves one by one. When I told them my name they all laughed. Then we played a game of carrying and passing energy from one to the other, a bit like Chinese whispers only the energy had to remain the same colour and density throughout as it was carried along the line. When it came to me it completely disintegrated and they all instantaneously sparkled like fireworks, laughing and whizzing around and couldn't be controlled by their elders. The dark light in the small room glowed purple with their exuberant energy zinging with joy. The elders thought it would be best if I left and visited them another time, which I did.

"You were privileged on that occasion to witness something very unique, were you not?", the female Arcturian prompted.

"Yes indeed, it is something I will never forget. I was privileged to watch an elder transcend to the next dimension." I said.

"Yes, he had waited for you. Your visit was not by chance. He called you."

"Why?"

"It is not for me to say, but someday you will understand. For now, suffice to know you were and are special to him."

I remember when I met him he seemed very familiar, like a Father figure and I felt at ease with him. He was so pleased to see me and joked about many things. Our meeting was a very private affair held in a small compartment like an old-fashioned, first-class railway carriage. Suddenly after our joviality, he became serious and I watched him fade from his head down into a dense autumn brown mass, like a dry leaf escaping from a tree. I called out to someone to help him as I thought he was having a heart attack, but no one came and I watched his body condense into what appeared to be a crinkly, brown paper bag which burst spontaneously into flames and was eventually reduced to a pile of ash. I was shocked by the disintegration of his body, but I had the sense that his transcendence was glorious. Someone led me away leaving me with a heavy sadness, yet at the same time, a feeling of great victory. "Now you will prepare for tomorrow. Remember there is always a reason for action. The Universe never responds to a vacuum," she smiles as she glides away.

It is early the next morning and I wake to the sound of feet padding along the corridor and subdued voices in the kitchen. I trace the voices and find Mari and her team discussing final mission tactics over breakfast.

"Come and join us," Mari urges, "We're just discussing plans for the attack. Breakfast is over there. We'll leave in an hour. Ok?"

I nod and listen to their strategy whilst preparing a meagre breakfast. I am nervous, although I will only be a spectator in the plot. Soon we board the roadster, which has been chosen to give the impression of being owned by a wealthy business lady – Mari who is dressed for the part in high-fashion red shoes and a tight-fitting red suit. Her make-up is overtly sexy and her hair falls in dark curls over her shoulders. She certainly looks like a rich, sexy entrepreneur. Our driver, it seems, is a skilled marksman disguised as a chauffeur.

Also in the front seat is our communications operator who, at the flick of a switch has at his finger-tips all manner of dials and electro-communication gadgets ready to fire if necessary to safeguard the mission. He is masquerading as the second driver. Mari has a miniscule, hidden camera inside a brooch on her lapel, so that all the transactions can be viewed and recorded. The mighty little ladybird gadget is masked as a pin in her hair so that when she and her handbag are searched they won't suspect the little clip is an awesome weapon.

I am disguised as Mari's assistant, dressed equally convincingly to play the role of Madam's aide, in a blue tight-fitting two-piece suit and my long hair is curled and heaped fashionably on the top of my head. Everything is in place for the task ahead and when we pull up at the compound security gate we all automatically assume our characters. There is no doubt or hesitation displayed by the guards as we sail through the barrier with ease. Mari and I are taken to the Principal's office through a well-maintained hallway which conceals the school's true state of disrepair. The Principal Sister of the Order waits to greet us and wastes no time in displaying photographs of ten eligible young girls for sale and tells us her price. Mari inspects the pictures and asks to see the girls in person before agreeing to the fee. The Principal curtly nods and calls to another Sister who rushes away to prepare the girls in question.

A ray of sunshine lands on the desk accenting the girls' faces in a halo of light. My anger bubbles as I remember the fear, ridicule and hypocrisy of the cruel religious bigots from my own childhood. The beatings, the secret bruises, the mocking, the taunting of religious fanatics parading as Priests and Nuns and still it seems, it continues. Mari asks pertinent questions about the girls while we wait and I am glad when an assistant enters to take us to see the girls, dispelling my submerged memories. As we follow the Principal and the assistant up the wide staircase to the dormitory, Mari surreptitiously unclips the ladybird from her hair and releases it into the atmosphere where it instantaneously disappears. If all goes well the drone will seek out Marta, attach itself to her body and safely, avoiding human obstacles or otherwise, will transport her across the compound to another waiting vehicle where she will be driven to H.Q. As we enter the dormitory the ten girls are lined up against their beds with little suitcases pre-packed ready for the journey. They are clean and appropriately dressed uniformly in grey dresses, grey socks and black shoes. Their faces hold no trace of emotion and their eyes are dull and unresponsive, as though the life force has been sucked out of them by their futile existence.

Waiting in the car, Amrad, the technician has a good view of the dormitory and is also tracking the drone searching for Marta who is hiding under a tiny bed in another dormitory for younger children. The boy who bullies her is looking for her, a large stick in his hand.

"Oh no son, no you don't", warns Amrad, waiting patiently to aim the ladybird at Marta when she appears in his target range. Enki, the driver follows the action on the screen and is ready with his ray gun to leap into action if necessary. They watch the bully- boy creep stealthily around the room searching for Marta. Unfortunately, the bed under which she is hiding is very small and her bare feet are visible poking out at the end of the bed. The boy spies her and smiles to himself as he raises his stick in readiness to wallop her feet but she is too quick for him and rolls out the other side of the bed, as his stick whacks the floor. She dashes to the door but he follows and pins her against the wall. She flails out against him but she is much smaller and he is far stronger.

"Quick! Aim! Fire!" shouts Amrad seizing the moment to hit the target as Marta is splayed against the wall, but her legs are free and she kicks the bully in his testicles. He falls on top of her in shock, as the ladybird whizzes through the air and lodges firmly in his back, just missing Marta. She is horrified and stands aghast as the bully howls and screams in agony, not knowing whether to nurse his scrotum or dig out the thing that is stuck in his back.

"Oh no! Oh no!" gasps Amrad as he desperately fiddles with switches and buttons to free the ladybird, but the device is locked into the target and will remain there until it reaches its destination. Marta stares open-mouthed in disbelief at the boy as he rises in the air hauled up by an invisible force just as the door flings open and two young assistant Nuns dash in stopped in their tracks by the sight of the boy above them, flying across the room, like a ghostly apparition.

"Jesus, Mary and Joseph," the Nuns screech in unison, as they drop to their knees to pray, fearing that the wrath of the Lord has descended upon them.

"Hah! Ah! Put me down! Let me go!" screams the bully boy. His plaintive cries echo through the building and children taking a nap in the other dormitories rush out to witness the horrific spectacle. They are enthralled and delighted to see the arch-bullyboy kick and scream as he flies helplessly through the air. The excited throng, inspired by the magical party trick roars and hollers manically following the flying boy down the hallway, throwing anything and everything at him as pottery smashes on his head, splinters and crashes to the floor. Books are hurled at his writhing body, and hockey sticks and cricket bats thwack his dangling legs. The more he screeches, the more the mob attack. "I'm going in!" utters Enki to Amrad," alert the other team, we'll need assistance."

Meanwhile, the Principal and her aide, alarmed by the commotion, rush out to investigate, leaving Mari and myself to get the girls to run downstairs and escape in a waiting vehicle, "Go on girls" I say gently, "don't be frightened, there are no guards on duty and the Nuns are all busy with the hullabaloo, so the coast is clear!"

They immediately run, tearing off their school name tags their faces beaming, flushed with excitement at the promise of freedom. Mari rushes after the Principal, who takes out a black truncheon striking at the mass of children, revelling in the fracas, but Mari throws her to the ground and the wild bunch pile in on top of their cruel persecutor, beating, kicking and punching until her body lies lifeless in a pool of blood. Mari tackles the assistant and throws her against a wall, where she bounces forwards into the angry clutches of the mob who swarm over her like bees buzzing round a hive, until she is flayed to pulp. I sprint through the rabble to find Marta. My instincts lead me to a small broom cupboard and as I gingerly open the gloomy door a little head bobs down behind the brushes. I call her name, softly – "Marta?" She doesn't respond. I feel the heat of her fear in the tiny, enclosed space. A little hand clings to a mop handle and before she can object I scoop her up in my arms. Marta kicks and screams beating my back with her fists and I race downstairs with my troublesome bundle and dash through the door to drop her into the back of the car, just as Mari also jumps inside. Enki rushes to the driving seat leaving a pile of guards strewn on the forecourt. Children are now streaming out of the main building scattering in all directions.

"Don't worry about them, they will find their own way out. There's nothing we can do to help them, we've got what we came for," shouts Mari as she pins down the screaming, kicking Marta who is howling like a demented banshee. "Don't get too near her hair and be careful not to touch any open sores on her skin... Jesus she stinks to high heaven! Sorry, got to do this, it's the only way...!" Mari produces a tiny needle from her pocket and quickly jabs it into Marta's arm making her squeak momentarily before she flops into a sedated sleep.

"Ooh what's that?" I wrinkle my nose as a wet warmth spreads across the seat.

"Jesus! She's peed! The little wretch? Oh God!" scowls Mari," never mind, I suppose it could be worse!" she scorns.

"How are we going to clean her up?" I ask, horrified at the task ahead.

"We're not going to clean anything my friend, we now have Nanny Robots to do everything. No one nowadays does anything like that. You will meet Robo and Roba who will take care of her, we won't have to lift a finger."

I am amazed and delighted to learn that the gruesome task will be taken out of our hands.

When we arrive at H.Q. we enter through a brick wall covered in luminescent graffiti which lifts open at the flick of a switch and closes rapidly as we drive into a different internal car park on the ground floor. I stare at Marta's emaciated body and her pinched little face that is ingrained with dirt. Her lovely long eyelashes are glued together with white gunge and her nose is caked in a yellow crust. Her hair is a matted mess of infestation, alive with crawlies. She is a pitiful sight. Mari orders Enki to lift her out of the car and take her to the hygiene clinic, which he does, unenthusiastically, holding her at arm's length to avoid the smell and the risk of any infection.

"Oh and by the way, tell the Bots to shave her head- her hair is infested and so it's absolutely necessary in this case," she orders, "now we have to report to the Chief. You did some good quick thinking there girl!" she adds, slapping my back and ripping off her high-heel shoes." You know I wouldn't be at all surprised if our superior Alien friends knew what was going to happen, that's why they insisted you tagged along," she clicks her teeth and winks as we enter the conference room where a team is waiting to debrief us.

When everyone in the unit is seated, the Chief orders 'lights out' ready to play back the incident video. We all watch in silence and when we reach the part where the target misses Marta, Amrad begins to speak but is immediately silenced by the Chief. We watch the whole episode unravel but the Chief stops it at the point where the bully-boy sails out of the window.

"Ok Amrad, you missed the target, right? Not like you son!" declares the Chief.

Amrad opens his mouth to defend himself but is silenced once again.

"A target missed once is a target missed twice, but not in this case," the Chief says.

We all look at each other, puzzled.

"In this case the lovely little ladybird was implanted with a Corrical code to re-direct the target to a different location from ours, in other words someone in the team is working for the other side. Someone here is responsible for tampering with the ladybird system."

Everyone looks around suspiciously, wondering who the mole might be.

"As it turns out, missing the target was a good thing and our enemy have now acquired a piece of live ammunition- a great little bully-boy to groom for future exploitation. Well, good luck with that one I say!"

At that moment armed guards enter and the Chief nods towards a man seated close to him. The guards move in quickly and paralyse him electronically with a sophisticated Taser gun. The man flops to the floor and is quickly dispatched out of the room.

"Like I said someone was working for the other side, but not for long hey? This time we were lucky to be saved by quick thinking and improvised action, which saved the day and we now have the target safely in place ready for transference. Well done, young lady," he says, directing his gratitude towards me.

The team clap heartily and I am overwhelmed by their warmth for a non-transhuman civilian, after all, I was only doing my job and with a little bit of luck the mission was successful, but I don't expect anything less, because I am LUCKY!

MARTA

The sea writes its signature briefly in the sand leaving no trace, cleansed and ready for the next chapter of the next story to be rolled and unfurled as the tide draws in and out its timeless breath. A lifetime is etched on the oceanfront with each brave new wave rushing to the shore, quickly bowled away in one fell swoop by the hand of nature. Life is given and life is taken, as the 'word' is spoken without a token of regret. Well, that was the way of the world before everlasting life was for sale and before the promise of forever was invented. In the 'now' of the new invention of eternity, I sit watching a little girl sleep. She will not know the promise of eternity on earth, for I will take her back to a time of limited life, a time of a 'birth-life-death' a sequence invented for the human race. Of course, it's not the end of our story, for as the sea rolls in and out, our lifetimes roll on to our designated destiny and like the ancient rhymes, in Odyssey times, we will roll on 'til the twelfth of never'.

I sit quietly by Marta's bedside admiring her spotless, fresh face and her little pink bobble hat covering her shaven head. The Bots have done a great job of bathing her and dressing her in cute pink pyjamas. Her little body is wrapped in clean blankets and I am so grateful that she is safe. I am grateful to the Universe for trusting me to look after her and I want to stay immersed in this tranquil state of gratitude, resting in the quiet of my being, knowing that all action should be Divine Action and all action should be performed in and through 'love'; for love is a miracle and miracles are love in action. These thoughts are words I know from somewhere before, but I cannot remember where. Suddenly Marta opens her eyes and stares at the ceiling, before sitting bolt upright, feeling her shaven, smooth head underneath her bobble hat and tearing it off in disgust. Her hands roam slowly over her shorn crown and realising that her hair has gone, she screams and howls, jumping up and down on the bed like a crazed bobcat. Abruptly she turns towards me and attacks me head-on kicking, biting and shrieking with all her might. Mari runs into the room and pulls me free of her, tossing Marta aside. The child drops to the floor, pounding her fists on the carpet and writhing around in a frenzy as Mari whisks me out of the room and locks the door behind us; "Keep her locked in there for a while until she calms down. I'll be back later. Got to rush," she pants, throwing me the key.

I flop down with my back against the door listening to Marta howling on the other side, smashing the wood heftily with her fists and pulling at the doorknob, twisting it back and forth, crazily. I curl into a ball against the door in an attempt to shut out the onslaught and allow tears to flow. Where is my gratitude to the Universe now? Has it disappeared after such a fleeting flash of insight? I am ashamed to admit that Marta is too much for me and I want someone else to shoulder the burden.

"Please take her away!" I whisper as her screeching twists a knife in my stomach and anger pulses in my head. I hold myself back from rushing through the door and smacking her. But I remember from my childhood the humiliation. I know the sting of rough hands against bare legs. I know what it is to be dragged out of bed in the middle of the night and thrashed for no reason. I know what it is like to lie in bed crying from the smarting throb of whipped legs. I know what that is like and I *will not* do it to her! The yowling continues and I cover my ears. A friendly hand strokes my head and I look up to see a warm smiling face as someone helps me to stand saying;

"Come on you need a break from all this. The kid is safe so let's go get a coffee."

I allow myself to be led by the kind stranger into the kitchen where he sits me down at the table and busies himself preparing coffee.

"Thank you," I sigh," I'm sorry, I don't know your name?"

"Doctor Connelly," he laughs," I'm the ship's doc. So to speak."

"Thank you for rescuing me, I just don't know what to do with her. I have no experience of being a mother."

"Ah well, that is not easy my dear, none of us are prepared for parenthood and believe me when it hits you – it hits you hard," he laughs knowingly.

"Do you have kids?" I enquire softly.

"Sure. I have three. All grown-up now and I have the joy of being a Grandpa, but nothing prepares you for the hard road that all parents have to tread."

"Luckily it won't be for long, as I just have to take care of Marta for a short while until we return."

He nods sympathetically and hands me a welcome cup of coffee, adding, "You know, kids are a lot tougher than we think they are. Believe me, they are very resilient and so long as they know you love them, all comes good in the end!"

I smile, feeling the wisdom of his words, but I don't intend to be Marta's mother, only her guardian for a short time. The break is calming but suddenly the quiet is alarming. I rush out of the kitchen and pause before unlocking the bedroom door. The stench hits me as I step inside. The Doctor who has followed steps back in disgust and ushers me out of the room calling for the bots to clean up the mess. I will not forget the sight of Marta smearing her own faeces all over the carpet. Her lovely clean pyjamas are filthy and stinking. Stains all over the fresh bed sheets repulse me and I gasp for air.

"The Bots will take care of this trust me! Another good bath and scrubbing will calm her down and then I will demonstrate a little fatherly 'know-how'. Always remember, gentleness is your strength," he says confidently.

I sigh, I was not expecting such disgusting, primitive, savage behaviour and bury my head in my hands.

"Come on, this time I think we'll try something a little stronger?" He chuckles patting my back. "You see the child is not to be blamed. She doesn't know any better, she has been treated like a wild animal so that's how she behaves. We just have to show her the correct way of doing things and she'll soon learn. If you give kids a good reason for not doing something, they learn pretty quickly. But foremost she has to be taught with dignity and kindness. Those two attributes hold the key to developing high 'self-esteem' and is one of the greatest gifts we can bestow upon any child."

I am grateful for his kindness and his wisdom and the whiskey which I sip slowly, wondering how he is going to teach her what is right. After a while the Bots appear with a very subdued Marta, smelling sweetly of roses, dressed in a clean pair of pyjamas and sporting her pink bobble hat. She looks at me and hangs her head. The Doctor places his hands on her shoulders and leads her gently to a science lab saying,

"I'm going to show you something Marta. Would you like to see something amazing?"

"Amazing?" she repeats, not understanding the word.

"Yes, amazing means magical," I add.

"Look here and see this," he points to a specimen of faeces laid out on the petri glass, "Do you know what it is?" He softly enquires.

"Looks like a dump!" Marta laughs.

"And it is, you clever girl and do you know whose 'dump' it is?"

She looks at him quizzically.

"Well my darling, it's yours. It came from your body," he assures her. She stands back pulling a face. "Smells awful, doesn't it?" He asks. She holds her nose. "Well you see there is a reason for that and it's because the waste from your body is full of bacteria."

"Bacteeeria...?" she repeats.

"Yes, terrible, dreadful germs that make you sick!" I exclaim, following the Doctor's teaching strategy.

"Let's take a closer look shall we and see all those nasty germs," he utters emphasising the word 'germs'.

She obeys him and looks under the microscope and pulls back in horror.

"They is creepin' and crawlin' around like worms!"

"Yes, that's right!" affirms the Doctor.

"How come I don't feel 'em wriggling inside my butt?" She asks holding her bottom.

"Well we can't always see and feel things that are there because they are so small and hidden. We can't see our heart, but we know it's there, we can't see our bones but we know they're there. Like many things we just have to believe what others who know better, tell us."

"So when the Doctor tells you that it is dangerous to touch bacteria, you must believe him, or you'll get sick..."

"And die?" she adds knowledgeably nodding her bobble-hatted head.

"Well, maybe not die, but you could be very ill. Now let me show you a picture of a bathroom. The bathroom is a very special, private place where you can take extra good care of yourself. You see the bath where you can have a lovely time splashing around. The sink is where you can wash your face and clean your teeth and of course the toilet..."

"A dumpster...!" she shouts out loud.

"Well, yes if you like, a dumpster," he smiles.

"Didn't you have a toilet in the compound?" I ask.

"No, dumpsters were for the grown-ups."

"What did you use then?" I enquire.

"We had a drain."

"Let's just leave it there shall we?" the Doctor advises, "but you now know don't you Marta that you must never, never..."

"I know," she adds.

"You will be shown how to use the ... er... toilet," he states clinically. "I suggest you run along now and you can go and explore the bathroom," he urges.

I thank the Doctor for his kind authoritative teaching and take Marta back to our room to continue the instruction. I show her how to clean her teeth with a supersonic gadget that has a laser beam to penetrate plaque and hidden germs. Marta says it tickles and that she likes the minty taste of the toothpaste which is automatically dispensed on the brush. Afterwards, we replace the gadget in the sanitary unit where it is hygienically sterilised. I show her how to wash her face by placing her head inside a protruding plastic face mask situated over the sink, which purifies the pores, cleanses the skin, steams the face, dries it and then moisturises it. She likes the smell of the rose scented soap and I teach her how to use the toilet and clean herself with the latest sanitation gadgets.

"Wow, a real dumpster of my own!" she croons, "I bet Billy, bully boy, 'aint never seen one of these?" She chants dancing around the bathroom but then, suddenly, she slumps to the floor screaming and crying.

"What's wrong? What's the matter?" I try to hold her writhing little body.

"You is nasty...you is nasty bitch!" she howls.

I am at a loss to understand her outburst and try to cuddle her but she thumps me in the stomach and runs to a corner and crouches down sobbing. I approach her quietly crawling on all fours, like approaching a wild cat in distress. "Just tell me what is wrong." I whisper stroking her arm. She stops wailing for a moment and stares directly into my eyes whimpering,

"You is cruel, 'cos you gonna take me back and sell me! You is doing all this to get me ready for the traders! I hate you! I hate you, 'cos you is white shit!"

I stifle a shocked laugh. On the one hand I am so relieved that she doesn't want to go back, but on the other, I am appalled that she could even think I am going to sell her!

"No one is going to take you back! No one is going to sell you to anyone, not the traders, not anyone!" I say firmly, holding both her hands in mine. It suddenly occurs to me that no one has explained to Marta why she has been brought here and I carefully sit her on my knee and tell her that I am going to look after her for a while and that we are going to have adventures together, but she has to learn to behave.

"Are you gonna be my Momma?" She asks softly.

The question stumps me as I hadn't thought about my role with that depth of responsibility.

"I aint never had a Momma before!" She sighs, hiccupping back her sobs.

"Er, well, er...well I suppose in a way I will be like er... guardian Mother."

"I gonna call you my Momalu!" She shouts, standing up and folding her arms.

"I expect you feel hungry now?" I ask not quite knowing how to respond. I had undertaken the mission understanding it was for a short duration of time, not involving an emotional tie. I take her hand as she looks up at me with new trust and certainty and follows me down the hall. I am happy that she has calmed down and is taking an interest in her new surroundings as we enter the kitchen. "What's this?" she asks, picking up a half empty can of lemonade. "Can I try it?" she wheedles.

"No," I answer and she scowls but I quickly add," no, only because someone has already been drinking it. You never know it might have germs on it!" Marta quickly drops it on the floor,

"I'll get you another one to try," I add trying to avoid any further confrontation. She smiles and tries to snatch the can out of my hands. I make her pick up the one she has thrown on the floor and clean up the mess from the small spillage and then I hand her the fresh can, making her take it slowly.

"Now say thank you," I prompt.

"Why?" she asks.

"Because it's polite and it's good manners and you say 'please' when you want something."

"Ok, thank you, please I want that can!" she demands.

I smile and give in showing her how to open the can and drink from it but the lemonade is fizzy and spills down her chin, and the bubbles go up her nose and she coughs and splutters.

"Drink it slowly," I caution.

Her second attempt is better and she declares she likes it.

"Now what would you like to eat? I enquire.

She shrugs her shoulders looking around the room for suggestions.

"What is your favourite food," I ask.

"I aint got none!" she sighs.

"I haven't got any," I point out correcting her, but she quickly retorts,

"Then why's you ask if you aint got none?"

"No, I have, but what I meant was…!" I leave the grammar lesson for another time. "I know, how about spaghetti animals and alphabet letters in tomato sauce?" I ask, remembering Nursery food from my childhood.

"What is spuzgetti?" she queries, "What is alfibetti?"

"Look I tell you what, I'll make it for you and then you can try it. OK?"

She nods walking around the kitchen picking up objects and inspecting them. She picks up an orange sniffs it and bites into the peel but puts it down quickly. I give her an apple and she bites into it and throws it on the floor, so I make her pick it up and show her where to put the rubbish. I order the computer to produce the food and it sifts through old-fashioned food recipes from a different era and manages to find the dish. Within seconds it appears, piping hot. I show Marta how to sit down at the table and she shuffles uncomfortably until she can reach the cutlery which she bangs on the table until I stop her. I place the spaghetti animals and alphabet pasta with tomato sauce in front of her and point out the little animals and the letters. I demonstrate how to dip her spoon into the sauce and guide the spoon to her mouth.

Just then Mari enters and as I turn my back on Marta, the bowl crashes to the floor. Pasta is plastered everywhere and Marta's face is covered in red sauce. She is too eager to get the food into her mouth and impatiently dives into the bowl with both hands splodging the pasta everywhere and plastering her face with sauce. Mari is angry and lunges towards Marta to slap her, but I step in automatically and stop her. "Bots, Bots, where are the Bots? Cleaning action needed!" shouts Mari in a temper, "just look at this mess. The brat needs to be punished!"

"No! No! No want the Bots!" screams Marta in a fury, stamping on the pasta, spreading the mess further over the kitchen floor.

"Take it easy Mari, she's only a child, and a damaged one at that," I interject.

"No want the Bots! No want the Bots!" Marta screams stamping her feet.

The Bots enter and quickly spring into action and I steer Marta away down the hall to our room and take her into the bathroom.

"Show me. Show me what a clever girl you are to clean yourself," I say, getting a grip on my tolerance level which is slowly diminishing. She looks at me as though I am stupid and proceeds to go through all the motions I taught her earlier. She has a few problems unbuttoning her pyjama top but apart from that she does a good job of cleaning herself and dressing in clean pyjamas.

"What are these called?" she asks examining the floral pyjamas.

I repeat the word and she sings,"Pyjamies, pyjamies, jarmies, pretty jarmies."

I am happy she is happy but I sigh, fearing the long road ahead for both of us. I am comforted by the fact that it won't be for long, my mission will soon be completed.

"Are you still hungry?" I ask, wondering what to give her next that will cause the least chaos. She nods as she sits on the floor. I relax on the bed and beckon her to join me. She obeys, tentatively unsure of the bed, as she has no experience of high-tech sleep pods but she inches up next to me and I put my arm around her, which she allows. I recite a list of options of snacks which she might like and that she can eat with her hands. She opts for chiplets and chocolate. This time in the kitchen there are no dramas but Mari watches from a distance with her colleagues, ready to pounce into action if Marta is naughty.

With trepidation, our first bedtime routine begins. The temper tantrums from earlier have left her exhausted but I am confident that she can handle the necessary sanitary requirements. When she returns from the bathroom I ask her to get into bed but she looks at me quizzically and scratches her pink bobble hat.

"What is it?" I ask, forgetting she doesn't know how to get into the pod. I watch her crawl underneath it.

"No, darling, come on out. Let me show you," I say as I climb into the pod which has remote controls that monitor everything as you sleep. I turn it off so that she isn't afraid and Marta watches as I snuggle under the covers then copying my move, scampers in quickly beside me. Her little body is shaking and I put my arms around her to make her feel safe and she cuddles me tightly.

"I know I'll tell you a bedtime story, shall I?"

"What's that?" she questions.

"Well, it's a story that children like to hear before they go to sleep."

"Why?"

"Because...well they just do. Er.. let me see, what about Goldilocks and the three bears?"

"Is it a true story?" she sits up with wide open eyes.

"No, it's a story which means it's not true but children, like you,..."

"What's it about?" she interrupts before I have time to explain.

"Er...it's about a family of bears- Mummy, Daddy and baby bear who live in a house in the forest."

"Bears have a house all to themselves?" she questions.

"Are you going to listen to this story or not?" I say firmly, my patience tested again. She doesn't reply and listens quietly as I tell the story and at the end asks:

"The baby bear has a Mummy and Daddy. Where is my Mummy and Daddy?"

I look into her sad little face and explain that her Mummy and Daddy are waiting for her and I am going to take her to live with them very soon. She cheers up a little and then asks:

"Until then are you my Mummy?"

I smile and nod, a little embarrassed.

"Momalu," she states, "You is my Momalu for now."

"Ok, I'll be your Momalu, but now you have to go to sleep," I try to get up but she clings to me. "Alright, I'll stay for a while. I'll sing you a lullaby." I begin to sing softly and she pats my face saying, "I'm trying to get to sleep, quit the noise!"

I stop singing and smile, feeling a strange sense of belonging and new-found contentment having been assigned a new role, which I hope I can accomplish successfully besides which, I figure it's not long before we leave for the past, but right now in the present, I am lucky to be 'Momalu' and not just Lucky!

BUILDING BRIDGES FOR TOMORROW

I wake early, my body aching having laid in one position all night, I was afraid to move in case Marta woke. I gently ease my arm from underneath her body and tip-toe out of bed as a little voice shouts:

"Why you is creepin' round like a cat on heat?"

"What?" I exclaim, shocked by her language.

"Why you is creepin'…?

"Yes, I heard you the first time!" I mutter.

"Is Jesus my Daddy?" she asks sitting up defiantly.

I pause, half wanting to laugh and half dreading the barrage of questions so early in the morning. I ask her what she means by 'cat on heat' and am relieved that she's only repeating a phrase she heard the older girls say.

"Is Jesus my Daddy?" she asks again.

"Why do you ask that?" I yawn, wanting desperately to go to the bathroom.

"Because every morning the Nuns is singing 'Jesus our Father' and we all sing 'Jesus our Father,' so is it true? Is he my Daddy?"

"Well in a manner of speaking, I suppose he is everyone's Daddy," I reply unconvincingly.

"So, it's not true dammit? I knowed it! I knowed it! I is hungry."

"I *am* hungry," I state, emphasising the 'am'.

"You as well?" she questions jumping on the bed, at which point Roboticca, the housemaid enters with a pile of clean clothes for Marta which she places on the bed and engages the child in conversation while I visit the bathroom. On my return Marta is screeching and hollering as Roboticca attempts to forcibly remove her pink bobble hat.

"It's alright Roboticca, she can leave it on for now. Thank you." I reassure her, attempting to soothe the situation as the Robot leaves, disgruntled that her task has been thwarted.

"Look at these lovely clothes to try on. What would you like to wear?" I ask, laying out a wide selection for her to peruse. She looks at me strangely when I hand her pants and is reluctant to put them on, but I persuade her to wear them, explaining that everyone wears underwear.

"Even Jesus?" she asks reluctantly.

"I am sure he does." I say, realising the 'Jesus' threat must have played a large part in the discipline regime at the compound.

"Look at this lovely pretty dress. Would you like to wear it?" I ask.

"No!" she replies curtly.

"These trousers, I want to wear these trousers like boys, so that I can punch everyone, like boys do!" she yells jumping up and down.

I sigh, thinking the day has hardly begun and already I want a rest. "Not all boys go around punching everyone!" I state firmly, but she isn't listening, as she is busy wrestling with the trousers and a matching blue jumper. I hand her dark blue socks and trainers which she doesn't like, but I show her how to put them on and she is quite pleased with the overall effect, admiring herself in the mirror, stating, "son of a bitch, I gottcha now!" as she takes a fighting stance holding her fists up to an invisible opponent.

"Look my love, that's not a nice thing to say," I add, gently.

"Do you think I'm pretty?" she asks innocently, admiring herself in the mirror.

"Of course you are, all little girls are pretty!" I declare.

"No they aint! Sister Mary Agnes, she is real ugly an' Marsha says she's a mean cooking custard!"

"What did you say?" I gulp. But she runs out of the door racing towards the kitchen followed by an almighty crash and an angry voice screaming:

"Look where the hell you're going, you stupid little brat!"

I rush after her just in time to see her crash into Mari and land in a pool of milk and cereals. Beads of milk drip from Marta's new blue jumper as Mari roughly scoops her up shouting:

"Now look what you've done? You clumsy little idiot! Can't you teach her better manners?" she grunts shoving her, roughly at me, but Marta wriggles free and turns on me in an hysterical outburst howling:

"I can't love you! You is white shit! You ain't my Momalu!"

My heart sinks as Mari grabs her by the shoulder shrieking, "and I suppose you can't love me either because I'm Indian shit and you can't love Lee over there because he's Chinese shit?"

Marta retaliates in a frenzied fit of scratching, kicking and like a rabid dog bites Mari's hand, escaping through the kitchen door just as Doctor Connelly enters. Mari, infuriated by the vicious attack examines her hand. I try to explain to her that Marta defended herself in the only way she knows how, she has been treated like a caged wild animal, so she reacts like one and until she learns how to behave, we've got to find a way to deal with her vicious outbursts.

"Why the little bitch? You just wait!" Mari snarls aggressively, ignoring my excuses, while she allows the Doctor to examine her hand. He produces a gadget from his pocket, like a ball point pen and aims the beam at the wound, where the intense light cleans and seals the skin together. Within minutes the gash is healed. Mari is grateful but still fuming from the assault.

"That kid is dangerous!" she snarls.

"Children are not born dangerous," the Doctor says," it's what's been done to them that makes them so! Love begets love, hate begets hate, let's not forget that!" he says firmly as he leaves to find Marta.

Halfway down the hallway a young man comes out of the science lab and motions the Doctor to go in, where he finds Marta standing on a stool and is peering down the lens of a microscope saying: "these is bacteeeria, I knows 'cos the Doc showed me and they is real bad critters!"

"That's absolutely correct Marta," declares the Doctor, "well done for remembering!"

"I is good at 'membering, I member lots!" she asserts proudly patting her own head.

"Well I've got lots more to show you," beckons the Doctor," come over here?"

Marta jumps down from the stool and eagerly skips to the doctor who has a large hologram of a polar bear extending forwards towards her from a computer.

"What is this animal Marta?" he asks.

"A bear, a bloody big custard white bear!" she claims, stamping her feet.

"Well, yes he is quite big," smiles the Doctor," but do you know what he is called?"

"Arthur?" she guesses, studying the polar bear closely, poking her fingers at his face.

"Well, er... no - he is a she and she's a polar bear.

"Polar bear. That's a funny name?" She repeats mechanically.

"And what colour is she?" he enquires.

"Why she is fluffy white!" Marta exclaims assuredly.

"Ahah! Let's see if that's so? Let's take a real close look at her skin," adds the Doctor as he zooms in close beyond her fur, "now what colour is her skin?"

Marta stares in wonder and amazement at what she is seeing.

"Well?" probes the Doctor.

"It's black! It's black, it's cooking black!" she exclaims.

"Yes, a polar bear might be fluffy white on the outside but its skin is really black! Isn't that amazing?"

"Sure, bloody, cooking custard is!" she chirps.

"Now I have something else to show you, come over here," he urges, trying not to laugh at her language. She sidles over to a counter to where the Doctor holds out a small, sharp gadget and she watches carefully as he pricks his finger watching a tiny blob of blood appear on a minute glass tray. "What's this?" he asks.

"Blood, yuk!" she grimaces.

"Yes what colour is it?" he questions.

"Red! Red! Bloody blood is red!" she chants.

"Can I see what colour yours is?" he asks calmly, but she is afraid and steps back.

"Look it doesn't hurt!" he coaxes, but she hides behind the counter and he calls over an assistant who obliges and they both show her their samples of blood. "See his blood is also red. Your blood is red. The polar bear's blood is red. Everyone has red blood. So really Marta we are all the same. It doesn't matter what colour you are on the outside, we are all the same inside. So poor Momalu is sad when you say she is white shit and by the way that's not a good word and neither is bloody and neither are the other bad words, so I don't want to hear them again, OK?

She nods and hangs her head and says," like bloody and shit and..."

"Yes all of those, you see we don't need them, do we? We have lots of other lovely words we can use instead and good little girls who are clever can use better words, to show just how clever they really are!"

"Yes Sir!" she says stamping her feet to attention and saluting in an ungainly fashion.

"Anyway, who told you that white people are...?"

"Shit?" she exclaims and then holds her hands over her mouth, remembering that word is banned. "Bella, at the compound says white people are sh... you know that word- so you can't love them, and she really don't like white people at all because they hurt her real bad!"

"Well now we know that not all white people are bad and we know that black, white, pink, yellow, are all the same inside- isn't that right Marta?" he asks. Marta nods her head slowly and he takes her by the hand saying, "now what do we have to do? What do we have to say to Momalu?"

"She's not white sh...poop!" she solemnly declares," and she's got red blood!"

"Well yes, but when we have hurt someone's feelings we have to say 'sorry' and that's what we have to do," the Doctor says as he escorts her to the kitchen.

In the kitchen Mari and I discuss plans to take Marta back to the past. I am eager to know the details, but Mari explains that there has been some kind of delay and it may be a few days until the all clear is given to make our way to the secret underground teleportation unit. She suggests that meanwhile I use the time wisely, to teach Marta manners and the correct way to behave and also how to read and write and generally integrate her into 'normal' living, otherwise she would have to be locked up. I agree to try my best to teach Marta and keep her out of trouble.

A tall man enters, who is a transhuman - I spy the implant chip in the back of his neck. He greets Mari warmly and looks at me quizzically.

"This is Olav," Mari smiles, introducing him almost shyly.

He is polite and pleasant sounding with a gentle foreign accent. He says his homeland is Russia but that he has defected and doesn't want to talk about it. He and Mari seem close and I am curious about their relationship tentatively enquiring if they are 'together'. Simultaneously they laugh and Olav replies: "Sure yes, together why not? We are together a lot, a lot of times, yes."

Mari laughs again and explains, "you come from a time when relationships were very different. People got married and generally stayed together all their lives because they had limited life-spans. Now people have multi- lifetimes and are re-generated over and over, so they can have many marriages and lots of relationships. Our lives here in the future are not the same as yours from the past."

I understand and smile, wondering if people store memories like they used to, or do they wipe out old memories to make way for new ones with each new life-span they acquire? The pair huddle in a corner furtively whispering before they beat a sneaky retreat, leaving me alone in the kitchen to ponder many things - the first of which is to formulate a timetable to teach Marta the basics, before Mari locks her up. How do I teach her in a fun way? How do I prepare a very special little girl for her important life to come? Strange to think that her future lies in the past? My quiet is disturbed as the Doctor and a very subdued small person enter.

"Marta has something to say to you," announces the Doctor, nudging her forwards. She steps gingerly towards me, casting her pretty eyes downwards and mutters, "I'm sorry!" She bursts into tears, spontaneously throwing her arms around my neck. I gulp back my own tears and momentarily we cling to each other, somehow feeling an enormous bridge has been crossed and we are safely together on the other side. She looks up at me and says,

"I know I ain't got to say shit, or cooking custard or any bad words anymore and I'm sorry for calling you white shit, because you ain't white shit because we all got red blood and white fluffy polar bears have black skin? Ain't that so Doctor?"

The Doctor smiles and we all laugh together and he hands Marta a bar of chocolate which she admires like a special prize, then tears into, like a hungry bear cub.

Down the hallway a commotion breaks out. Men are rushing up and down shouting orders to one another. The Doctor tells me to stay put while he investigates. I hold Marta's hand and she grips mine tightly while we wait anxiously. The noise rises and the sound of an explosion downstairs echoes through the floorboards. I become a protective mother hen, and I hold Marta close, very much aware that she could be taken from me at any moment. Mari is not around to help and I feel vulnerable without her.

"We need to move NOW!" shouts the Doctor raising his voice above the din as we scuttle out of the kitchen. I am shocked to see a massive gaping hole where our bedroom used to be and a huge mound of bricks and rubble piled high, smouldering with dust and plaster hanging in the air like a white cloud. The Doctor whisks us up to the top car park where we are ushered into an aero-car. Thomas our driver is there, ready to zoom off. The Doctor hands me a small contomitom, which is like a cell phone, computer, communicator all in one gadget, explaining that I can reach him with the device and that Thomas can be trusted. We are going to be taken to a safe place where we must wait until we are called. Shockingly, he tells me that under no circumstances am I to trust Mari, as she is working for the other side. He hands Marta a chocolate bar and reeling, I thank him as we zoom out across the crowded sky, dodging Sky-riders and air transporters and large air freight trains. Marta stares out of the window wide-eyed as she has never flown before and is transfixed by the sky and the cloud formations and the cities built in the skies. Thomas is a skilled driver and steers us out of the clogged sky highway to a less cluttered sky track. I ask him quietly where we are headed and he shakes his head explaining he is not allowed to say but reassures me that we will be safe.

"Are you ok?" I whisper to Marta who has a chocolate-stained mouth and sticky hands.

"I sure is, I'm fine and dandy!"

I smile at her language and the phrases she has learnt at the compound from old movies. She was never taught how to speak or communicate her feelings from first-hand experience; she only knows what she has seen and heard.

Marta enjoys the ride as though it's a fairground treat. I am happy she is happy, showing no sign of fear as perhaps only a child can, when danger threatens. I am shocked about Mari, and yet in a way maybe not, as she always seemed too harsh with Marta and the appearance of her Russian boyfriend just before the explosion was somehow suspicious. Their behaviour was odd but I trusted her and I shudder to think where Marta would be now if Mari had taken her. I push all negative thoughts away and concentrate on the journey, mentally preparing myself for what I might have to deal with when we arrive at our destination.

Suddenly we enter a dense cloud blotting out the bright sky and Marta is a little troubled to be completely shrouded in white mist. She asks what clouds are made of and I attempt to give a scientific explanation but she doesn't understand so I tell her a magical story about fluffy white clouds, white unicorns, white horses and white doves.

"White polar bears," she adds, "that are really black, aint that somethin'?" I laugh and she laughs too as she urges me to carry on the story while we continue our journey. Slowly her eyelids droop and she is soon asleep, her head resting on my shoulder. I love the way her little mind latches on to a whole new realm of make-believe and I watch her comprehension of the world expand with delight as more and more novel ideas excite her imagination.

"We are going to land soon, Mam. I suggest you brace yourself for the landing," commands Thomas, "hold on tight to the little one!"

Marta stirs and shivers as she wakes in the cooler temperature of the late afternoon. The light is dimming as we prepare to land.

"Where are we?" Marta asks sleepily.

"I'm not sure," I reply hiding my apprehension, "but I tell you what, we're going to have a great adventure. You and I are going to have lots of fun!" I hold her close to shield her from the bumpy landing, feeling her hot sweaty hands clutching mine as we drop quite fast and our stomachs almost jump into our mouths. Jerkily we land on a small flat circled area amid scrub jungle. Thomas hands us a couple of blankets and a flask of water explaining that someone will come and take us to a secret homestead in the forest where we will be safe for a while. I plead with him to stay with us but he is in a hurry to leave, fearing for his life. We watch as he scampers back into the little areo-bus and see him take off and disappear into the clouds. Marta shivers and asks,

"What is this place, I is cold?"

I open my mouth to correct her grammar but decide we have more important things to attend to, like surviving.

"It's a forest," I tell her.

"Like in the story of the three bears?" she asks.

"Yes, that's right, a quiet lovely forest with lots of trees!"

"And these is trees?" she queries, looking around "It's awful bloody noisy for a quiet place!" she exclaims.

I smile, realising she has never heard the wind in the trees, the call of the birds or the rustling of the grasses but I watch her easing into her new surroundings, with a growing calm acceptance. I suddenly remember the contomitom and decide to call the Doctor. The signal is weak but luckily I get through. He is glad we are safe and assures me that someone will come to lead us to the homestead but it would be best to hide and take shelter in the forest, just in case there are any hiccups. I take his advice, wrap Marta in a blanket and lead her into the forest where the trees weave a safe canopy. The Doctor's voice trails in and out of signal as we hide inside the forest, "Look" he says, "what you have to remember is that, this short time you have with Marta, is like taking small building blocks and constructing a bridge to lead her into her future. Take small baby steps each day to build her knowledge of the world around her and train her how to deal with all situations with confidence and strength. You must help to fortify her personality and character through good experiences and although, when she returns to the past, it will be as a new-born, all that you teach her will remain inside her memory cells. You are her vital link to her successful future-remember you are building a bridge for her tomorrow!"

His voice fades and in the supreme quiet of the moment, a vast realisation rests heavily on my shoulders. I should be fearful, perhaps even horrified at the situation, but somehow I am not. The Doctor's words inspire me to succeed and if they have planned this all along then, I must be grateful and feel lucky to know that 'all will be well, as all is well as all shall be well' as a fourteenth century Nun once wrote.

"Momalu I is hungry!" whines Marta.

"I know love, we'll soon have a wonderful feast when they come for us, come on cheer up, I'm not called Lucky for nothing you know!"

"Momalu, that's a silly name!" she giggles and we laugh together, snuggling into the blanket in a thicket under the spreading branches of the trees.

WHEN YOU'RE NOT LOOKING BUT SEEING SIDEWAYS – YOU SEE THE WORLD AS IT REALLY IS!

"When are they coming?" Marta whines for the hundredth time.

"Soon," I reply, trying to hide my concern.

"You said that last time!" she moans.

"I know but really, I'm sure it won't be long now!"

The light is growing dim and we're both hungry and cold. We have been waiting for hours, to Marta it must seem like an eternity. I wonder if they have abandoned us or if something bad has happened to our rescuers. I flop down by a wide tree trunk and put my head on my knees, crying out internally to the Universe for help. From far beyond a voice in my head replies:

"Just when you think all is lost, all will be found. Remember the Universe responds to positive thoughts. Trust is a matter of opening your heart to abundance. Abundance of good possibilities will happen, just believe. Every time you face a risk, you increase your ability to trust and every time trust is built, you increase your own self-worth. Trust is the link between the mental world and the physical. Trust, believe and receive. Expect only the best to happen at all times- and it will! That is all."

The voice fades as a bright light shines on my face. I can't see the person holding the torch but his hand over my mouth is gentle as a male voice whispers,

"Shh... don't make a noise. Come on, we haven't got time to waste. Here little one, let me carry you, have this?" he hands Marta another bar of chocolate which she attacks voraciously. I can't see his face but still instinctively I trust in him to lead us safely to our destination. We hurry through the forest forging a path across the dense overgrowth lit only by torchlight. We don't speak and even Marta is quiet as she munches her way through the large chocolate bar. The stranger is nimble and quick and I have great difficulty keeping up with him, clinging desperately to his sleeve for guidance. He warns us to shield our faces from the branches and straggling brambles as we force our way further into the dense forest. Sharp thorns scratch my legs and spiky bushes prick my arms as I fight my way through the overgrowth. We race on and on and I can hear my heart thumping in my chest. There is no let up and the stranger keeps up the pace even with Marta on his back. He gives the impression of a well-trained, very fit soldier as he navigates his way almost effortlessly through the thick undergrowth.

Occasionally the moon peeps through the trees and casts shadows before us and for a few moments I can make out my footing but then it disappears and we are plunged back into darkness. Eventually, I feel him slow down until we stop by a tree.

"Wait here!" he cautions, as he puts Marta down gently beside me and we watch him disappear into the brush. Marta clutches my hand with her sticky, chocolate fingers as we wait. The stranger is stealthy and swift, returning like a black- panther stalking prey in the jungle. He moves close and momentarily I feel his strong chest, hard as a rock, as he bends forwards to whisper:

"Watch carefully what is about to happen. You need to understand the mechanics of our hideout." He shines a torch on a small black box and presses a red button instructing us to observe the 'R.M.C. which stands for Reflective Mirror Camouflage'. The farmstead is completely covered in reflective mirror material, which is heat, water and gunfire-resistant. This kind of camouflage was used centuries ago, especially in Antarctica, where reflective mirrors shielded portal entrances to underground cities and hid secret Alien bases built in the ice. Now our R.M.C. is much more advanced and we can camouflage larger areas with a fool-proof protective film. Watch as the cover unfolds and then we can proceed. Inside there is electricity to light and heat the place, but once the shell is down, the space is vulnerable to air patrols, heat sensors and living vibrations. You are only safe when the canopy is up. Watch as I pull it up, see the film reflects all the trees, birds and sky-line all around as though there is nothing there."

As the moon slides out from behind the clouds, the stage is lit for our performance and we view the mirror effect in action, marvelling at its effect. The little farmstead completely disappears folded in the reflective camouflage material as though a magician has reclaimed the forest with his magic and then miraculously, with the flick of a switch, the farmhouse re-appears. Marta gasps at the conjuring trick and is unusually, lost for words as the stranger guides us into the unprotected building. As soon as he secures the outside seal, he turns on the lights and we see each other properly in the light for the first time. He breaks the silence, "hi, I'm Ji," he holds out his hand and I shake it, gratefully.

"Hey, you is a soldier, but different!" chirps Marta, holding out her hand to shake his.

The soldier laughs acknowledging her observation. "Correct little lady. I'm a soldier all right, from Korea and I'm here to look after you for a short while, but you're gonna have to be a soldier too and take orders, understood?"

"Understood Captain over and out!" Marta salutes, clicking her heels together, like she has seen in old-fashioned films.

"Where did you get that from?" I laugh with amusement and relief.

"Oh sometimes we seed old war films at the compound an' I knows all about soldiers 'cos Sister Mary Gregory likes soldiers a lot. Sometimes they visited her."

I glance at Ji and he smiles shyly. "Well, I guess we better get this place ship-shape and you two must be hungry?"

"You bet! I is *real* hungry!" enthuses Marta.

"Well you can help me then," Ji declares, walking over to the kitchen unit.

I am thankful to be safe and I wander around checking the layout. It's only a small place, consisting of one large room with the kitchen opposite the sitting area, which turns into a bedroom where the sofa and chairs fold into beds. There is a toilet and a separate shower room and storage cupboards at the other end. It's very basic because, I suppose, people only use it as a short-term hideout.

"So you are sure we are safe here?" I ask.

"For a while, until they track us down, and make no mistake about it, they will, but it's my job to keep you safe. Ok?"

I nod and sit down, observing Ji transform packaged dried food into a real meal. It seems he is an expert at creating Korean cuisine from packets. I trust him. He seems genuine and very competent and there is a hidden kindness behind his dark eyes. Soon we are tucking into a wonderful medley of dishes and Marta is delighted to sample tastes she has never before experienced. I thank Ji profusely for his efforts and want to show him my gratitude by clearing the deck and washing the dishes but he says although the base is small, it is fully operational with hi-tech equipment which only he knows how to work. I graciously leave it to him and oversee Marta's bedtime preparation. She refuses to take off her pink bobble hat, so we settle down in our makeshift beds, fully clothed. We are very tired after the day's events but just as I am about to drop off to sleep Marta sits up abruptly calling out,

"I'm glad Jesus isn't my real Daddy!"

"Oh Marta, not now, just go to sleep!" I groan.

"Well I is!" she retorts.

"Am!" I correct, now fully awake. I can't help asking "why are you glad that Jesus isn't your real daddy?"

"Because Jesus lives in Heaven, right? So I wouldn't get to see him until I is dead! But having a real daddy here means I might get to see him one day. Will I get to see him Momalu? Will I?" she wheedles.

"Yes, yes you will, now go to sleep. I can promise you that one day you will have a wonderful father who will take care of you and love you very, very, much! Now go to sleep!"

Marta snuggles down underneath the blankets, satisfied with my reply and soon falls asleep. Ji hovers around continually checking gadgets and keeping a look-out and I fall asleep wondering about Jesus and Heaven!

In the morning we wake to the sound of breakfast being prepared and I sit up quickly to see Ji laying the table. I am comforted to see his smiling face, knowing we are safe. Marta stirs as the smell of fried eggs wafts over us and she smiles, skipping out of bed to greet Ji. She seems completely at ease with him and helps him with the food. We take our time over breakfast as there is no rush to do anything, we can't even go outside but nevertheless Ji chivvies us along:

"Come on ladies we've got work to do!"

"Work?" we question simultaneously.

"Yes, you didn't think you were here for a holiday did you?"

"No Sir!" shouts Marta, getting into the swing of army role-play.

I am a little reticent to jump to commands and am cautious about what he wants us to do. When the breakfast area has been cleared, Ji instructs us to stand in the middle of the free space where he sets up an obstacle course with chairs and a table and a few saucepans for us to jump over along with two pieces of rope. He explains to us, in army commando style what we have to do, repeating it twice so that we both understand the course. We hover by the door waiting for the 'go' signal. When Ji commands us to start, Marta races ahead loving the challenge. I am not as enthusiastic about playing party games and allow Marta to win. She is a natural athlete and very supple.

"What do you think you're doing?" Ji bellows at me. "This is serious! She has won because you didn't bother! For that slovenly attitude you are going to complete the course another ten times and at speed otherwise you will have to do it ten more times. Do you understand?"

I nod, shocked by his yelling and harsh tone. I hate every second of this stupid game.

"Do you understand?" he bellows.

"Say yes Sir!" whispers Marta, nudging me.

"Yes Sir!" I shout. Marta pushes me forwards.

I begin the course at an even pace which isn't fast enough for Ji and he hollers at me to go faster and faster until I trip over a bucket and he tears into me for being clumsy. Marta is embarrassed and distressed at my incompetence, so for her sake, I continue. When Ji is satisfied with my performance he makes me run on the spot and I begrudgingly declare:

"I can dance and dance for hours, but I hate running!"

"Get on with it!" Ji is not tolerating any excuses.

"Just do it Momalu...please?" Marta gently encourages me to complete the training.

"Right soldiers, now I'm going to turn up the heat and I don't just mean the temperature. This training is for your own safety. You don't know what or who is waiting out there and you have to be vigilant at all times and well prepared to meet any unforeseen challenges. So let's take this seriously. It's not a game to while away the time. Do you hear?"

I am exhausted from the exercise and Marta looks puzzled. Ji has told us that the base is fully operational high- tech, but we are not prepared for what happens next as the light changes and the temperature rises to sweltering point. The sitting room completely transforms into a blistering, humid jungle accompanied by all the sights and sounds of jungle insects and creatures.

"Ok you guys, you've got a two-minute start, get running!" I begin to jog lazily on the spot and Marta copies me.

"I said RUN..!" Ji bellows, "Your life depends on it!"

Loud thuds vibrate the ground and the sound of crashing through the brush alerts us that something terrifying is chasing us and as I take a quick peek behind my heart jumps into my mouth. A huge dinosaur is hurtling towards us. I grab Marta's hand as she shouts,

"Holy shit! Mary Mother of Jesus save us!"

Together we flee for our lives, hot breath searing into our backs and the dinosaur's heavy feet close on our heels. I trip as Marta runs on ahead and a hefty thwack strikes my back. I am falling and I see Marta running back to save me just as the lights switch back to normal and the jungle fades into the walls of the living room. The heat returns to its original temperature and the virtual blow on my back doesn't hurt, because it isn't real.

"Ok, at ease. What did you learn from that experience?"

"Dinosaurs are bloody big fuggers!" pants Marta.

I squirm and Ji tries to hide his laughter. "Well, yes that's true but you both need to know that when I tell you to do something, you have to obey immediately and not half-heartedly because your life could depend upon it. So if I say RUN, you bloody well run! Got it?"

Marta looks at him surprised at his language and then looks up at me as if to say, if he swears so can I!

"You weren't quick enough!" he points at me," if that was real then you'd be an acid mess inside the dinosaur's stomach by now!"

"Urgh...!" grimaces Marta adding, "but I ran back to save her, I aint not gonna let any big, damn cooking dinosaur eat her!"

"Ahh, yes, that was thoughtful, but I never want you to do that again. You always have to save yourself first. It's the primary law of survival. Understood?"

"Yes Sir, over an out...but...?"

"No buts Marta I mean it! Got it?"

Marta nods, scratching her bobble hat. I guess her hair is growing back and in the jungle heat, it would be itchy. I offer to take it off for her but she refuses and stands by Ji waiting for further orders.

"Your Xian Zu training should have taught you better and to obey orders promptly!" he says pointing a finger at me again. Marta shuffles uncomfortably from one foot to the other, upset that I am receiving another blasting.

"Now for something completely different. I want you ladies to wear these." Ji indicates some heavy winter clothing. "Unfortunately, we haven't got a set of Icelandic gear small enough for you Marta so we've got to improvise."

The temperature grows icy-cold until it is minus forty degrees. The ice-patrol gear is very warm and the black goggles soothe the intensity of the ultra-white landscape. Marta is cocooned in a small seal-skin suit and her pink bobble hat peeps out from underneath a thick bear-skin hood. Her goggles are a little large but are adequate to shade her eyes from the penetrating glare of the bright sun on the ice. Ji holds a snow scooter for Marta to climb on the front, while I stand on the back ready for take-off. It is engine driven and the controls are very basic with only an on/off switch. At Ji's command, we slowly rev into action and I love the sensation of gliding along on the ice. Miles and miles of white tundra lie ahead with nothing but undulating white hills in the bright sunshine gleaming in the distance. Marta sits still in the front and I wonder what she is thinking. She is being given the most spectacular experiences to help enrich her understanding of her world.

Suddenly, ahead, I spy figures. I can't quite make out what or who they are, but as we glide nearer, I see a large Mother polar bear with two babies, obviously hunting for food. I stop the scooter and wonder what to do. A voice in the ear-piece of my hood affirms; "That's right. Just stay still. The Mother will sniff the air and will know you are there. Polar bears have tremendous capacity to smell prey from about forty miles. After a long hard winter they can attack without warning. Stay calm." It's a real thrill to see the bears in their natural habitat but at the same time I am fearful that the Mother may want to eat us. The cold, now that we have stopped, bites into my face and breathing the air stings deep in my lungs. Marta remains totally still and I am impressed by her self-control. For a few moments the Mother bear is motionless, sniffing the air with her black nose pointed in our direction. Suddenly, without warning, she gallops towards us, kicking up the soft snow into small white puffs of clouds behind her while her little cubs race to keep up. I remain still, as ordered. Then the voice instructs: "Slowly take out the flare in the front pocket of the scooter. Count to three then pull off the top and hold the flare up high. It will scare off the bear."

I follow the instructions carefully. When the bear is so close that I can see into her eyes, I pull the flare, releasing the explosion into the air. The bear halts and looks around, sniffing the dangerous fire sparks shooting up into the atmosphere. She pauses then turns, leading her cubs in the opposite direction.

"Phew! That was close!" I whisper and the voice in my hood responds, "you did good! Well done!"

Suddenly the snow melts back into the sitting-room walls, while the light dims as the heat returns and the cold wind dies down, as Marta and I clamour to shed our warm suits.

"Did you know polar bears have black skin, Ji?" she asks, flaunting her newly acquired knowledge, seemingly unaffected by the dramatic escape.

"No little lady, I did not!" he replies.

"Well they do an' that's why it don't matter what colour we is because we is all the same!" she says, in an authoritative manner.

"Quite right!" Ji laughs.

I collapse on the floor exhausted from the nervous strain of the experience and I can't help but ask why we have to go through training which isn't pertinent to our situation..."I mean a Dinosaur for heaven's sake and a Polar bear?" Ji glares at me angrily and sighs, taking his time to reply.

"This training is devised for you to understand, from your time zone, how to manage the difficulties which might lie ahead, today, tomorrow or next week- so don't question it! We don't have time for me to explain the whys and wherefores, Ok? Now for your third and last test we're going somewhere different again."

"Where?" shouts Marta jumping up and down excitedly.

"You'll see," answers Ji as he plays with the controls manoeuvring our setting to an idyllic paradise island with beautiful white sands, palm trees swaying in a gentle breeze and a tranquil, azure blue sea gently lapping at the shore. Under a palm tree there is a luxurious lounger and a towel spread out on the sand. Marta and I change into swimsuits but she still refuses to part with her pink bobble hat.

"What's that on your arm, Momalu? Looks like a cooking squito bit ya. I know, 'cos them damn things sting so hard and yah have ta spit on the bites, like this!" She spits on my arm just above the wrist and rubs it in with her finger exclaiming, "there that's done good now!"

I smile and thank, her trying to remember where and when I was stung, but I can't recall. It's definitely a mosquito bite, as Marta points out, but I have no memory of being bitten. When I was regressed to my younger self, they told me that any birth marks, cuts or bites would probably not be erased by the process. It looks like I have brought a mosquito bite with me into the future from my past! I rub the bite which Marta has so kindly spat on and try to concentrate on the next exercise.

I look around and see coconuts scattered under the trees and as Marta picks one up to examine its strange shell I explain it contains milk, that people drink and that they eat the white flesh inside, too. She wants me to open it, so I search for something to puncture the shell, wandering near the edge of the thick, tropical bushes to explore the ground for a sharp stone and a larger one to use as a hammer. Looking back, I can see that Marta is happy splashing about in the sea so I continue my search, going a little deeper into the jungle. I can't find anything suitable but then suddenly, as I scour the ground, a pair of lime- green eyes, with vertical black, split pupils is gazing back at me. Slowly I take in the pre-historic scaly skin and the vast jaw line with its rows of uneven sharp teeth. My Xian Zu training urges me to stay calm and back away slowly. I know that crocodiles are most active in the late afternoon and tend to be sleepy during the early part of the day. I am also aware that a fit human can outrun a crocodile, especially if you run in a straight line. I suspect this croc is lying on a nest of eggs and won't move unless provoked, so I back off carefully, keeping alert in case she springs. Luckily she stays on her eggs and I am able to get back to the shore. I look up and down the beach for Marta, but I can't see her. Panic rises in my stomach and I race to the water where I last saw her playing. Desperately, I shout her name running up and down the shore. Then my heart almost stops - her little pink bobble hat is floating on top of the playful white waves.

I jump into the water and swim frantically towards her hat. The water is beautifully clear with bright coral dancing in the underwater current and little electric blue and yellow fish darting in and out of quivering sea anemones. Suddenly, I spy a little body twisting and spiralling, turning somersaults underwater like a little fish in an aquarium. I swim towards her and quickly pull her up to the surface where she splutters and yells:

"Oh poo! You spoilt my fun!"

I hug her to my chest, my heart thumping in relief.

"What's the matter Momalu, why is you ballin' like a cry baby?"

I don't reply and kiss her wet cheeks. "Ah you is a sloppy Jo!" she laughs wiping away the kiss. She swipes her bobble hat from the surface and plonks it on her head dripping wet, and as the seawater streams down her face, we both laugh.

The sea disappears and the palm trees fade into the walls as the sitting room returns to its normal setting. Marta and I change and re-appear to be questioned by Ji.

"So what did you learn this time Marta?" he queries.

"I can swim and I likes swimming a lot!" she declares demonstrating her swimming style with her arms flailing the air.

"I didn't know you could swim!" he smiles.

"I can! I can and under the water! " she confirms and we all laugh at her confidence.

Now Ji turns his attention to me and asks, "What did you learn about yourself this time?"

"Well, I learnt to stay calm and believe in myself and not to let fear take over." I reply sheepishly.

"Yes, Xian Zu teaches that fear is a reaction which inhibits the immune system and changes blood chemistry in the brain, affecting emotional and bodily health. Fear has no part to play in a happy life. Love and happiness hold the key to all," he says adding, "the smallest change in your mind can make the difference between life and death. When you came face to face with the croc, if you had allowed your fear to change your vibration, the croc would have attacked you, but because you remained calm, you did not disturb the creature."

I understand the lesson.

"Now these lessons you have both learnt today are for a purpose and you must remember them when you are faced with danger. Do you understand?" he asks.

We both nod and Marta blurts out," I'm hungry!" easing the tension of the moment. Ji lightens up as he takes on chef duties and encourages Marta to help. I take out the Doctor's contomitom to check out world news and other information which we might find useful but Ji prevents me from using it as the enemy could suss out our position from its signal.

In no time, Ji competently produces another delightful meal and afterwards he selects a lovely old musical, especially for Marta. It's 'Annie' a story about an orphan child and Marta loves it and gets up to join in the singing. Her favourite is 'the sun will come out tomorrow' and long after the film is over she keeps piping up with the chorus making it difficult to calm her for bed! Eventually in the stillness of the night, all is tranquil and I drift off to sleep, but I am soon woken by Ji, gently shaking my shoulders his finger to his lips. He has spotted movement on the radar and is worried that it might be the enemy. I get up, silently and watch the screen with him. The night infra-red camera picks up bushes rustling in the wind but Ji is not satisfied that we are alone. The super sound system is amazing, picking up every little detail and I listen with bated breath as the undergrowth crackles sporadically, as though someone is masking their footsteps. A bush swishes close by and I gasp, as Mari comes into focus with Olav by her side, both carrying guns. Ji's body stiffens in readiness to deal with the enemy, but although they sense we are close, the mirror camouflage is very effective and for the time being shields us in our safe cocoon.

"What are we going to do?" I whisper.

"Well firstly, we are going to stay calm and not let fear obstruct clear thinking, remember?" he whispers.

I nod and try to steady my shaking hands and tell myself that I am not afraid. I follow Ji's instructions to prepare a small bag with food, water and two small blankets, while he identifies an escape route. He says that the handful of prowlers are heading back into the forest but it won't be long before the main team arrive with more finely tuned equipment to suss out our hideout with lasers. He explains that we will have to leave quickly before they return so that we can get a head start and get to a lake that channels out to sea. "I have traced a small boat which we can use, so don't worry. We'll be fine," he assures me. I trust his words, realising our training earlier that day was in preparation for just this kind of dangerous situation.

I gently wake Marta and quietly organise her for our escape, doing my best to prevent her from breaking into her new favourite song, 'The Sun Will Come Out Tomorrow'. When we are ready, Ji leads us out into the cold night air. We are not allowed the light of a torch and I cling to his sleeve as I guide Marta, through the undergrowth, holding her little hand tight. She thinks the adventure is another game. It's odd that when I don't want to make a sound, any sound that I make seems to echo louder than ever and the more I try not to snap twigs, the more I do. Marta's little feet, however, hardly make a sound as she walks over the tangled forest floor and Ji with his jungle training, steps soundlessly through the scrub. Ji is ultra- cautious of all sounds and movement and every few yards, he motions us to stop while he steals ahead to check that the coast is clear.

Near an opening in the thicket, he motions us to wait and disappears into the brush. Suddenly, from behind me, a gloved hand whips around my neck and clamps over my mouth. Marta is snatched up in someone's arms and a rag stuffed under her nose, instantly making her flop like a rag doll. My arm is twisted up behind my back and I am afraid to move in case it snaps like a broken twig. I am pushed forwards and begin to move, propelled by the man behind me. I keep calm. The training has taught me that fear interrupts clear thinking and that I must not react to the brutal treatment. A rough gag is shoved into my mouth and secured tightly with a rope around the back of my head. My hands are locked with plastic ties against the base of my back. It's difficult to stop shaking from the cold night air and the shock of Mari standing directly in front of me picking up Marta's limp arm and letting it drop to make sure she is sedated.

"Well, we meet again my friend. Seems she's not such a wild animal, after all!" she says sarcastically pointing to the unconscious Marta, "you must have done a good job. Anyway we'll soon see. Take her away!" she orders.

I try to break free but Olav holds me in a tight grip. I can't bear to see Marta hanging limp like a rag doll. I know she will fret if I am not there when she wakes.

"What about the soldier?" enquires Olav.

"He's nowhere to be found, but he can't escape our radar," answers the guard.

"Micro beam him if necessary," orders Olav. "What are we going to do with her?" He asks Mari.

"She's not part of the bargain. She's quite inconsequential to the action. If we leave her here tethered to a tree, she'll starve to death. It really doesn't matter, we won't be responsible for the deed," whispers Mari.

They agree and push me to the ground where a tree stub punctures my cheek. Blood spurts out over my chin and a sharp pain stings my eyes as my body is brutally pushed against a tree trunk and tied to the base with my legs forced together and bound with thick rope.

"Sorry my dear to leave you like this, but I'm sure you understand that orders are orders. No hard feelings. It was nice knowing you!" Mari sneers. "Come on let's get out of here!"

Olav and Mari lead the way and a soldier carries Marta. Another soldier has gone to track down Ji and in the awful, terrifying moment, I fear the worst. I am helpless, alone and injured. I should be quaking with fear but strangely a hot, throbbing anger shakes my whole being.

I will not let my life end like this! I will not give in! I will not allow them to take Marta. I will survive!

The saliva in my mouth is drying and the back of my throat is sore. The cut on my cheek is painful, the circulation in my legs is being cut off by the tight rope, my arms and shoulders are aching and I feel dizzy... but something light, something bright shines from the bottom of a deep dark well. It glides upwards from a cavernous pit lighting the blackest, bleakest corners. What is this glow? Where is it coming from? How is it giving me the inner strength to fight? "I believe...I believe in the greatest power that is. I believe in the Supreme, Almighty Force and Divine energy of love," I call out to the Universe in my mind as I am engulfed, bathed and consumed by sparking crystal beings who guide me gently away from my body into the bright light of Eternal Energy and I pass into a strange dream-like zone.

From somewhere out in the cosmos I return. The tingling in my legs worsens as the rope is cut from my ankles. The rag in my mouth is yanked out and my mouth twitches as I move my jaw up and down. My hands are freed and the dried cut on my cheek has stopped stinging. I am back in my body. I am alive! Ji helps me to my feet searching for broken bones and is relieved to find I have no major injuries. I involuntarily hug him and he is embarrassed. "Marta? Marta? Where is she? I have to get to her!" I cry.

He places his hands firmly on my shoulders saying, "Calm down little lady. Calm down."

"But I have to get to her!" I plead, pulling away from him.

"It's all right, she isn't in any danger. They won't hurt her. We will get her back. Do you remember what you have been taught? Think positive and don't be afraid. Expect only the best possible outcome and it will happen."

But in that moment of sheer distress, being separated from my little girl, I can only see her face and feel her warm little hands in mine. I have to find her. I can't waste another moment dithering around. I have to search for her! As I try to run my legs crumble, but Ji catches me in time before I fall into the brambles.

"Now look, you've got to listen to me! Focus! What has the training taught you?" he prompts as he places me carefully on the ground.

"Not to be afraid," I whisper.

He nods and sits beside me with his hands on his knees.

"Strategy! Think strategy. Seeing sideways." He says.

I am not sure what he means. I know he is right that if I allow panic to take over, I will lose everything but I am not sure what he means by 'seeing sideways' and I urge him to explain.

He smiles and sighs, looking up into the night sky and asking," Are you OK now?"

I nod and follow his gaze up into the clear, starlit sky where no light pollution disturbs the atmosphere and the cosmos is a vast kingdom of glistening planets. He points to the stars whispering, "Look up there, what do you see?"

"Beautiful stars," I answer.

"Yes, looking straight ahead you see what is in front of you, but what do you see sideways?" he questions.

I think it's a riddle and I turn sideways to look at him, but he turns my head back to the stars and repeats the question. I try to see what is in my periphery vision.

"I see you, but not clearly, I mean I know you are there but...,"

"Precisely! You know I am here you can sense me and feel my presence even though my image is blurred. Correct?"

I nod, checking out his theory, feeling his presence, rather than looking at him directly.

"Marta doesn't have to see you directly. She feels you. She senses you and she knows you will come for her."

Unexpectedly tears fall and I feel exhausted with overwhelming love for the child. "You know how sometimes when we're not looking for something and then we find it when we had forgotten we had lost it?" he laughs rubbing his hands together.

I know that feeling well, but I am not sure I remember what it is that I have forgotten to remember and momentarily my mind goes blank.

"You see when we are not looking, we see things more clearly- that is when we don't worry about all our problems, the solution appears right in front of our eyes. It is when we step back from the world that we can know our true reality."

I listen to his wise words and he calms my fears while he shares his plans to save Marta. He takes out a packet of biscuits from his rucksack and hands them to me. "I'm not hungry," I answer disdainfully and he laughs carefully opening the packet slipping one out to examine it saying:

"On the outside an ordinary-looking ginger nut biscuit, agreed?"

I nod, I'm really not interested in snacks when I have other pressing matters on my mind.

"Mmm, well that's where you're wrong! Each biscuit has a microchip explosive device inside the centre. When you throw it like this... (he mimes throwing a disc) it picks up energy from the air and speeds up to hit the target and then – it explodes! There's enough here to wipe out the lot of them!"

I am amazed at the technology and ask him how he is going to find them in the forest. He explains that he already knows where they are through a tracking device on his wrist. His plan is to sneak up on them just before dawn at the point in a clearing where he believes they will board an Airbus.

"Have you ever seen something out of the corner of your eye and when you turn your full attention to it-it's gone?" he asks.

"Yes," I laugh," I know that feeling. Perhaps it's the shadowlanders lurking. We see them when we're not looking."

"Right!" he says," "You will be a shadowlander."

I look puzzled, not following his train of thought.

"See this device? He holds out a small black box that looks like an old-fashioned camera," Yes, it's like a camera. It takes a picture of you and projects it up to half a mile away, like a hologram. So we take a photo of you and from a strategic point, you will appear in their periphery sight line as though you are actually there. Just at the point when they turn to look at you, press this button and you will disappear.

You will do it several times from a safe vantage point, distracting their attention in the opposite direction from where you are situated. They will not understand what is happening and because they are being extra cautious to protect their prize, they will be drawn to investigate, at which point, I will explode the biscuit bombs and rescue Marta. You will wait for us at the safe spot until we can all escape together. Got it?"

I nod, amazed at the plan. I hope with all my heart that it works. Yet again I am astonished at the techno gadgets. I would never have thought that a small box could create a hologram convincing enough to attract the enemy's attention, but then my mind wanders back to 9/11 when the Twin Towers were attacked and later it was suggested that it had been a holographic illusion of a plane crashing into the buildings while bombs had been placed in the buildings weeks before the attack. Already, back in those days, techno tricks were being hurled into the world arena and played to entrap the masses into subservience to the New World Order.

As we set off stealthily through the woods, the moonlit branches weave silver patterns on the forest floor lighting a gleaming trail through the undergrowth. Momentarily we pause as Ji listens to the forest sounds, making sure we are headed in the right direction. He smiles, whispering:

"Think lucky and you will be successful!" he encourages, patting me on the shoulder.

He doesn't have to tell me that, since I already know- because I am Lucky and always will be!

⊰⊹⊱

HOLES IN MAPS LEAD TO SOMEWHERE!

I am exhausted! My head is pounding, my heart is racing and my body is wet with nervous perspiration. I struggle to fight the night-terror from seeping into my being and my mind battles with so many 'what ifs?' jumping from one outcome to another with the ultimate scenario of Ji and I being killed. I have to prevent myself having negative thoughts. I gulp back the bitter taste in my mouth and conjure up, from deep within, the 'goodness energy'- hearing my voices spurring me on whispering:

"Purposefully send out good, compelling currents into the universe and like great waves in the ocean, they will swell and return, rising up stronger than before."

I know they are right and I want desperately to believe them. My legs obey my brain and keep on jogging through the bracken but my heart is in shreds. I have never felt the separation pang of a mother from her child before but I know, now, that there is no pain like it! I hadn't bargained on being so attached to Marta, but somehow it happened, like falling hopelessly in love when you least expect it. I had aimed to be professional and detached in my mission but emotion took over my senses. Now I am racing through a midnight imbroglio, a mess of entanglement and fear of physical harm. The small bombs that will explode will maim and probably kill Mari and the soldiers and I have to remind myself that it is necessary in order to rescue Marta. The voices in my head return:

"Violence is in itself evil, but 'Just' retribution is divine reckoning. Righteous wrath is celestial justice!"

I am comforted by their guidance and pause for breath as Ji halts to assess our position. He leads me to a spot behind a large tree where I can watch the operation, unseen by the enemy and operate the holographic gadget. He shows me where to aim and how to work the stop/go system. When he is sure I understand the procedure, he explains that a flashing green light on the box will indicate that he is ready for me to spring into action and I am not to move once the bombs are fired. From my vantage point, I can just make out the enemy camp and hear muted voices. Ji disappears and the waiting is tortuous. My hands shake and I am afraid I will set off the device by mistake. My eyes are glued to the box watching for the green light as my mind grapples with the possibilities of the technology and the fact that holograms can appear as real as reality itself. As reality is multi-dimensional, the possibilities are boundless. It's no wonder that people can be fooled, in the holographic realm, into believing anything they are shown. Ji, explained that the Japanese are leading the way in holographic technology and they have discovered that there are seven hierarchical dimensions in our universe, each with a unique frequency and that planet earth revolves on level four. He also clarified, that understanding the frequency in which humans exist, aids the scientists in their quest for greater and better holographic techniques and as everything in our world is vibration, then altering frequencies to suit design becomes easy. He explained, in great detail, the technology so that I would have a better understanding of the little black box.

Suddenly the green light flashes and I jump into action. I press the 'on' button and an invisible beam projects a moving image of me in the bushes. I wait just long enough for the enemy to see movement in their peripheral vision. As they move towards the image I switch it off. I watch the soldiers stop and look at each other, puzzled. As they turn to go back, I switch it on again for a few seconds until they respond, then switch it off. Three soldiers run around looking baffled, meanwhile, Olav has them covered with his gun and Mari is standing by Marta with her ray beam at the ready. Ji signals me to press the switch again and I watch as the soldiers, this time with Olav and Mira, chase my holographic image. By the time the mirage disappears, the enemy has moved away from Marta and Ji speedily and skilfully hurls the mini flying saucer biscuits into the air.

Every disc seeks out a specific person through heat sensors and as the targets are struck, the sky splinters into shards of yellow, red and orange like a magnificent firework display. I shudder as Mari, Olav and the soldiers burst into flames, screaming in the dense night. Through the firefly flashes and the burning ashes, I spy Ji lifting up a small bundle and scurrying with it into the bushes. Soon he is by my side with Marta in his arms who raises her head to look at the burning bushes in the distance and comments dreamily:

"Are we gonna have a barbeque Momalu?"

The smell of burning flesh in the cold, night air is very pungent and her comment makes me shudder.

"Quick we have to get out of here!" orders Ji and he throws Marta over his shoulder in a fireman's lift as we plough our way back through the woods heading in a different direction. I am so relieved the plan worked and deliriously happy to have Marta back.

The hours plod by as we gouge our way through the thick scrub jungle. I watch the sky slowly change from muddy black to watery silver, then into streaks of baby blue flashes flooding the horizon, until golden rings tip the leaves as the sun rises and we finally sit down to rest in a safe place in the bright morning light. Ji gives Marta some water to sip and takes out a packet of biscuits. I jump at the sight of them but he laughs saying," don't worry these are the real macoy!"

"I is tired Ji! Can't we go back to the farmhouse?" whines Marta, rubbing her legs.

"No, we're going on a little boat, out to sea!" he declares enthusiastically.

"A boat? A boat?" shouts Marta jumping up and down.

"Shh!" cautions Ji," we don't want to make a fuss now, do we?"

Marta shakes her head, still bubbling with enthusiasm and I feel warm inside to see her so happy. She doesn't remember being kidnapped and just thinks it was all a bad dream. After the promise of a boat ride Marta is in a better mood to tackle the last part of our journey and we all push a little harder to reach the lake. On our way towards the edge of the forest a large, desolate, broken-down barn comes into focus and Ji instructs us to hide while he goes to investigate. Marta and I hide in the brush where she takes a small stick to uncover an ant's nest.

"Do ants go to heaven?" she asks.

"I'm not sure, why?" I reply moving us quickly away from the nest.

"Cos I just stamped on plenty!"

Ji rushes back and gives us the 'all-clear' signal and we dash towards him and Marta forgets about the ant dilemma.

"It's ok," he says," it's only a derelict robot cemetery."

"It's what?" I query.

As we walk on he explains that robots, cyborgs, half-machine and half-human computerised androids eventually become obsolete as better products reach the market and as they are self-replicating computers, especially the Xenobots, they continually reinvent themselves and cannot be destroyed, so they are dumped in desolate places where they are left to rot.

"Such places are nick-named 'robot cemeteries' and I suggest you don't go in," he advises, but I am curious about this sad resting place for robots and beg him to let me just peep inside.

At first, Ji refuses but then agrees but absolutely won't allow Marta near it, so they go on ahead while I gingerly open the dilapidated barn door. The sight is horrendous! I wish I hadn't been so insistent and curious, but I need to see for myself what a future 'robot cemetery' looks like. A shocking mountain of human-looking machines are precariously piled high in stacks all around the barn, with some bodies stuck at the bottom still struggling to break free, screeching incoherent words. Congeries of half-dead cyborgs blinking with bulging eyes and mouths gaping open and shut, like gasping fish out of water, call out randomly. Pieces of broken limbs are strewn everywhere. Robot heads with half-eaten faces have rolled into dusty corners glaring vacantly into space. Headless mechanical torsos spring up and down constantly in an eternal death dance while half-limbed cyborgs stumble around, falling to the ground as their mechanisms whir and grind at double speed to hoist them back up. Some of them look so real, calling out recited phrases with human voices, 'Yes Sir! No Madam! How are you today?' There are human-looking sex dolls sitting with legs akimbo, placed purposely in provocative positions, by the robot refuse men as a joke. The plaintive cries of dead technology echoes around the barn and I leave, slamming the door on Dante's inferno, unable to forget the haunting images.

Hastily I catch up with Ji and Marta and the look on my face tells all. I know Ji wants to say-'I told you so!' but he doesn't. As the morning light brightens we can see the forest edge dipping towards a beautiful lake and we know the last push is in sight. Marta hums her favourite song,' the sun will come out tomorrow' as she races down the slope to the water's edge. Ji makes sure the coast is clear with a small tracking gadget he carries in his pocket. I look for the boat but Ji explains that we have to follow the lakeside until we see it tethered to a wooden docking post, so for a while we walk calmly by the water's edge listening to the gentle sound of the waves lapping against the pebbled shore. Rounding a corner across the lake, we spy a small cream and blue boat with a tiny blue canopy.

"Is that it? Is that our boat?" cries Marta, delighted to be the first to spot it.

Ji nods and orders Marta and me to wait with his bags while he boards the boat. We sit and watch as he nimbly darts through the trees, jumping over logs and hurtling through branches until he reaches the small vessel. I watch him search the area, to see if anyone is watching and then he unties the rope and jumps in. The boat has a small motor which he starts up without a key but another small gadget fires the engine. He is constantly watching the lakeside in case he is being followed.

When the boat draws near, he beckons us to get as close as possible but we still need to paddle through shallow water to clamber on board. As soon as we are safely inside, Ji wastes no time in steering out of the lagoon towards the open sea, where the atmosphere changes. The air changes to a cold, damp salty mist that clings to my long hair. The waves are choppy, mercilessly bouncing us up and down as we forge ahead. Marta loves it at first, she thinks it's like taking a fairground ride, although she has never before experienced one, but then she begins to feel sick, so I make her a little bed inside the hold where she lies down although it doesn't help much. The grey sea folds in and out in a timely rhythm and as we speed towards the horizon, where the grey sky and grey sea meet. The hours drag and it seems we are no nearer to the edge of the world than when we first set out.

As we sail into unknown waters, Marta manages to rest, while Ji and I become almost hypnotised by the endless pulsing of our boat on the choppy sea. Neither of us are hungry but down in the hold where Marta is sleeping, I spy a cabinet and to my mischievous delight, discover a bottle of Malt whiskey. Ji has three little beakers in his bag and I unfold two and pour a couple of shots saying,

"Come on, it helps prevent sea sickness!" He smiles wryly taking the beaker and downing the shot in one go! I pour another and we begin to unwind. Gradually the sun sinks behind the horizon in a final splash of glory as the grey shades of the afternoon diminish in a golden halo with pink and purple flashes of twilight magic, heralding the darkness beyond. Perhaps it is the whiskey or maybe the great sense of freedom and the intimate brush with danger which unites two people in a magnetic urge to be close- I cannot say, but the gentleness of his hands and the warmth of his breath make me curl my body into his and we kiss. "Freedom is worth the journey," he whispers as we embrace again.

"Ah no! You two aint doin' that yukky stuff are yus?" moans Marta as she pops her head up from the canopy, "I seed Sister Mary

Margaret kiss Father Malone, I did, so did Celia and she said that Sister Mary Margaret was going to have a baby. Momalu, are you gonna have a baby now?"

Ji and I quickly part as I assure Marta I am not going to have a baby.

She stands between us, complaining," What's that smell? It smell like Sister George's medicine bottle."

We laugh and come together in a group hug as the moon comes out to play hide and seek among the starry clouds. Marta feels well enough to chomp through a whole packet of dried biscuits, while Ji and I peck at some savoury snacks to soak up the whiskey. We don't sleep much and Ji spends most of the night steering the boat, although I take a turn to give him some rest, until the morning strikes a clear shot of watery white light across the skyline. In the far distance we spy land and as the early morning mist clears we make out the outline of a small island, home to a minor range of hills.

"Is that where we are headed?" I enquire.

"No," Ji replies, "it's a smaller island, not too far away. There's a map somewhere..."

"Here it is," pipes up Marta, handing him the map. Ji gives the wheel to me to steer while he shows her our position and where we are going, but the spot where we are headed isn't there! Instead Marta's little finger peeps through a hole in the map. Ji laughs saying,

"Well I guess this is where we are going!" he holds up her little finger to examine it, "looks like holes in maps do lead somewhere after all!"

Marta giggles at his joke and feels much better in the calmer water. I have to admit that I am disappointed that the island is not where we are headed and we veer away from it heading further out to sea where the waves become choppy again and Marta has another bout of sea-sickness.

Time is endless. The water is endless. The sky is endless and the waiting is timeless. I am thankful that Marta manages to sleep and I wonder if it's the after effects of the drug they gave her, but she seems fine. The morning, the afternoon, the forever of the day eventually blends into twilight and the moon slides out from behind a solitary cloud, painting a silver pathway across the dark undulating ocean. A little tired voice whines in the dark," Are we there yet? I is fed up with the boat now! We done enough sea sailing for ever!" I reassure Marta that it isn't much further but Ji scowls as he knows it's much further than he dares to say. I place another blanket over Marta and stroke her head until she falls asleep and then climb back up the tiny ladder to stand by Ji. I dare to touch his hand at the wheel and he smiles a weary response. I ask him about his family in Korea and he explains that before the New World Order when Korea was a separate country, he was happily married with a son, but when everything changed and the Global Elite took over, he was conscripted into the army and sent to America and never saw his wife and son again. They were killed in an uprising, fighting for their freedom.

"I'm sorry!" I murmur.

Suddenly the engine cuts out and the little boat floats silently. Ji tries to fiddle with controls, presses buttons and pulls levers but he can't fix the problem. An hour passes as he attempts to repair the boat before he has an idea;

"Don't worry," he urges, "we have friends who will help."

I am puzzled and wonder how, in the middle of a vast ocean, friends would be able come to our aid? I watch him as he takes out another gadget from his pocket. It is blue and round with a glass domed front and has strange signs and symbols inscribed inside it. A magnetic pin spins in the middle, like a compass, as Ji exhales softly across the top of the dome making the pin spin crazily backwards and forwards as the vibration from his breath activates it.

"Look overboard," he instructs.

I stare into the black, murky water and see nothing but dark, swirling shadows surging up and down, but then, in the distance, far out under the waves I see a flash of silver and make out shimmering sea creatures gliding speedily towards us, like shooting stars and sparkling jellyfish in the moonlight. As they fly through the waves they illuminate everything around them lighting up the vast sea world in a magical ballet of thrilling acrobatic aquatics.

As one draws near to our vulnerable little boat, a webbed blue hand appears on deck, then another as the sea creature heaves itself up pulling its scaly, blue fishy tail behind it, which swiftly transforms into a pair of azure-blue legs as it steps on deck. I gaze dumfounded at a seven-foot tall human-like being with electric-blue, rubbery skin like a dolphin, a magnificent torso and athletic legs. It looks like he is wearing a deep blue diving suit. His head is bigger than a man's with piercing, hypnotic-blue eyes, thin closed nostrils and a reedy-thin mouth. Tiny white and pale blue crustaceans cover his head and drip over his forehead. I have never seen a hybrid mix of man and fish before and I am lost for words. He speaks to me telepathically with a lovely lyrical, lilting voice, as though he is singing an ancient song. He tells me his name is Marinos and to be calm and not to worry, as his aquatic people will help us. Just then, another webbed hand slaps on the deck followed by another and a beautiful woman with a fishy tail hauls herself up as her scales convert into perfect, feminine legs. Her skin is dolphin-like and lighter in colour than Marinos. She is regal, elegant and graceful with ballerina arms which float like wings as she speaks. Her body glistens with tiny diamond particles strewn over her breasts and pelvis like a designer swimsuit. Her face is stunning with sparkling blue eyes set in a shiny silver mask with a dark blue thin nose and silver narrow lips. On her blue forehead, two aquamarine leaf-shaped symbols hover over her eyebrow line and move slightly as she tilts her head to speak to me telepathically in a silver-toned singing vibration. I imagine her voice to be like the sound of the Sirens, who tempted sailors to their briny deaths. She tells me her name is Silmarina and her people the 'Aquamarinas' are friendly, have lived deep below the ocean before man was invented and will help humans in trouble, especially those with clean hearts .

As she speaks Marta wakes and clings to my arm, hiding from our Aquatic guests whispering:

"They smell fishy!"

Silmarina smiles and explains that her people ruled the waters long before humans took to living on the earth and once some of the Aquatics began to spend longer time on land, using only their legs to move, they lost their fishy tails and were stuck with legs forever. But the call of the sea, their true home, still pulls humans to the ocean.

"Is you a real Mermaid?" asks Marta, daring to peep out from behind my back.

Silmarina laughs and holds out her webbed hands for Marta to touch saying, "that is not our true name, but yes, we are a mixture of human and fish. Some humans evolved from our species and lost the ways of our magical kingdom when they became land-locked and imprisoned in the earth's seasons, experiencing lean times causing upheaval, destruction and war amongst themselves. Our people have always lived in peace and will always exist in a plentiful, loving realm. We live in a higher vibration than you earth people and you can only find us when we allow you to.

I sigh, wishing that existence was not always just about survival of the fittest and ask," I have heard that inside the earth's crust, there are also such kingdoms, is this true?"

"It is so. Our Aquatic people were the first beings to evolve and still live under the ocean. Some of our people became human, choosing to live on earth and others of our clan chose to live under the earth's shell."

"Ah, I see, so there is such a place as 'Middle Earth'," I say.

"If you wish to call it that, but it is more complicated and we do not have time for me to explain the existence of life under the earth, as we have to get you safely to your destination. In the meantime would you like to come with me to see a part of our underworld paradise?"

Marta enthusiastically agrees but then is afraid and I am also uncertain, as I am fearful of going deep under water, but Silmarina persuades us to take a trip in an aquapod. Ji encourages us to go saying that it will be some time before we arrive at the island so we should go and have fun.

It is hard to refuse, so Marta and I follow Silmarina. She conjures up an egg-shaped glass container with two small seats. It rises from the sea and rests on the surface while we climb inside. It is comfortable and we can breathe without masks. Silmarina places her arms around the pod guiding it carefully back under the water as we sink slowly down and down. Marta's face is a mixture of fear as we drift down into the dark water and awe, as fishes swirl around us in shoals to investigate our intrusion into their secret world.

As the water becomes clearer, the light of our aquapod shines a bright pathway in the dark depths of the deep, we are suddenly aware of lots of little Aquamarinas swimming and waving, next to us, welcoming us into their exclusive world. Little boy Aquas similar to Marinos perform acrobatic tricks diving in and out of rocks and riding on the backs of sluggish sea turtles, while little girl Aquas, as beautiful as Silmarina, dance and swirl waving white diamond wands which sparkle through the orange and pink coral. In the distance, we spy magnificent castle towers and turrets in luminescent shades of greens, blues, purples and yellows and arches of sea urchins waving as we pass. Massive multi-coloured blossoms swirl as our little pod glides by in the truly amazing fantasy kingdom.

Silmarina and her sisters steer our pod into an air-tight cave where she opens the door and we step into a fairyland of surprises and delights. Some Aquawomen are sitting on rocks with their glimmering, scaly tails occasionally flicking, intently watching us with kind appreciation. Other Aquawomen are walking around on their rubbery blue legs collecting bright flower heads in a fishy dish. Some children are playing running around on their little blue legs throwing wobbly plants to each other in a game of catch and some older women are knitting coral garments. Silmarina introduces us to everyone and they welcome us jovially, offering anemone juice to drink from pink and white conch shells. Some of the children bring us crystallised seaweed to eat and Marta is surprised that it tastes like candy. Then the Aquachildren sit on the rocks facing us in readiness to perform the most enchanting music. Some blow hollowed out shells like captivating flutes echoing through endless cavern chambers and some have stringed lyres made from finely tuned fish gut rippling like wondrous harps. Others sing haunting melodies in their sea world choir. Marta is enthralled by the performance and doesn't want to leave as we are led back to our pod. The children blow fishy bubbles which ping when they pop and Marta is delighted when one lands on her pink bobble hat. The Aquachildren follow us and as they dive back into the ocean, their legs transform into multi-coloured fish tails with shiny silver fins gliding through the rippling water. Silmarina is sad to see us leave but she says it is time for us to head back to the boat, which has been towed near to the island by the Aquamen. When we rise to the surface into the light of a new golden dawn, I thank Silmarina for our fantastic experience and we watch as the Aquamarinas quiver under the water, gliding back to their beautiful kingdom, leaving silver trails of white foam on the waves, in their wake.

Ji is happy to see us and informs us that we are just minutes away from our destination. I had almost forgotten that Marta would soon be collected and my mission would be terminated. Ji gathers our bags and Marta picks up the map poking her little finger through the hole saying;

"See holes in maps do lead somewhere and here is a pretty good, damn somewhere!"

Ji and I laugh, relieved to be on land once again. I am so grateful to be alive in the moment of our liberation, feeling the luckiest person to experience such wondrous happenings, having escaped to an idyllic island. Yes I am grateful to the Universe for it all and so lucky to have been chosen for the mission, and I regret nothing, remembering my whisperer's advice:

"Never let regret seep into your energy field, for all that is, is meant to be and all that is meant to be is driven solely under your command through your own magnetic, energetic, vision. Don't hide who you are from the world because if you do, your luck will fade. Point your compass in the right direction and luck will be your companion, for you are Lucky."

PUPPY LOVE

As we splash our way towards the shore I spy an old man sitting on a rock waiting for us. He has long, black, thin, greying hair trailing over his shoulders and a garland of pink hibiscus crowns his head. Around his neck hangs a string of black beads and animal teeth. He is wearing a long kaftan jacket made of raw, fawn silk over his white lungi pants. In his right hand he is holding a large wooden staff with a shrunken human skull on the top which rattles as he stands. Ji places his hands together in a respectful pose and Marta and I copy, as we greet the Chief.

"Chief Monduata," Ji addresses him respectfully, "we thank you for your welcome."

The Chief bows his head in return, thrusting the end of his large staff into the sand, in a display designed to show us that his land is our land and we, as his guests, are free to stay for as long as we want. His wise old eyes smile as he says, "when love sparkles, the whole world shines. Manathey... Welcome!"

From over the hill, a tribe of people meander down to the beach bearing welcome garlands. The children place a string of shells around Marta's neck and taking her with them, they run off giggling. It is a wonderfully joyous occasion and I am sorry that I don't have any gifts for them. Suddenly I remember the two blankets in my bag and I offer them to the Chief who accepts them gratefully. Ji and I are treated like royal visitors and the children embrace Marta and have taken her off to explore the island. A delicious feast is prepared in our honour with various meats, vegetables and exotic fruit wrapped in banana leaves and placed in a dug-out oven beneath the earth and left to cook for a few hours with hot coals heaped on top. Just before sundown the celebration begins when the drums beat and the fruit-cup flows.

"We have a saying here, 'Don't dance before the drums beat'" says Yumata, one of the Chief's wives as she laughs handing us some toxic, fermented fruit cup.

Everyone enjoys the fun festival and the bonfires crackle, shooting orange, yellow and red flames up into the dark night, as the sound of the sea gently sighs beyond. The children have a wonderful time playing until they fall asleep in their tracks and loving parents scoop them up and take them to bed. In the early hours of the morning we finally retire to a lovely mud and grass hut lent to us by Undata, another of the Chief's wives. Sleep is welcome and glorious. Sleep is perfect. Sleep is magical on the paradise island with the smell of freshly harvested grass and herbs wafting through the open shutters.

The next morning I wake in the sublime vibration of total peace and tranquillity with no commuting, shouting or arguing in prospect, just the joy of being alive. I wish I could stay in the state of nirvana forever, but a nagging voice in my head reminds me that I have a duty to return Marta to the past for she has a life to devote to her nation. Walking by the seashore with Myaka, another of the Chief's wives, she explains that everyone in the community has a purpose and a special function in the village; even the children have individual chores and animals to nurture. No one is left alone or ignored. Everyone is unique and extraordinary in their eyes. She explains that their community is situated in a dimension that is above the earth's fourth dimension and below the next higher fifth dimension. I don't understand how that can be, as I only know my existence on earth and ask her to enlighten me. She smiles as though she is talking to a child and pauses looking out to the azure blue sea curving around the white sandy cove and states,

"Everything in our Universe, as we know it, is pure vibration. On planet Earth there are many vibrations emanating from different energies. Some are good and some are bad. When you learn to vibrate on a higher frequency, you lift your spirit upwards and you can access other planes and other spheres where existence is based wholly on pure, undiluted love. So here in our paradise we are governed by love and you have been directed here to spend some time with us to experience it so that when you return, you and Marta will take loving energy with you.

"But how did we get here?" I ask quizzically.

"Your own good intentions and loving vibrations brought you here and when it is time to return, you will take only loving memories with you, to feed your spirits."

"What about Ji?" I enquire.

"He is your emissary and he must take care of himself when his duty is over" she says quietly.

I ask about marriage, love and relationships, as on earth it is an aspect of my life that I find difficult to manage. Myaka giggles saying, "we live, we love and we laugh!"

"That is wonderful but who decides on marriage and divorce and...?"

She looks puzzled, "it is very simple for us. There is no marriage, therefore there is no divorce. Everyone lives in a state of 'love'. We need nothing else.

"But don't you get angry, jealous or possessive?" I question.

"Why would we get angry when we have so much to be grateful for? Why be jealous when there is enough love to share? Why be possessive when we all own the very same?" she says simply.

Her words put me to shame and I am silent in the overwhelming truth of the moment. I, we, society have much to learn. "Do you know the colour of gratitude?" she asks quietly.

"I have no idea, I never realised that gratitude had a colour." I reply.

"Yes, all emotions have colours and gratitude is pink. Pink like the hibiscus in my hair," she says removing the flower from behind her ear. "Yes pink because it is a mixture of white and red vibration. White for purity, cleansing and healing and the divine spark of love. Red for life blood, passion and birth. Together they create pink, which is a magical vibration for fun and for showing gratitude."

I take the flower and place it behind my ear to show my gratitude to her for sharing her wisdom. In the distance, I spy Ji helping the men with the fishing nets and watch from afar as the skilled task is tackled as a joint effort for a shared bounty, realising the feast of the day will depend on their expertise. The peace of the moment is disturbed as Marta, wearing the native costume and flowers in her hair, runs towards me crying.

"What's the matter? What's wrong?" I ask, taking her into my arms to soothe her sobbing.

"They won't play with me. They won't let me stroke the puppy!" she bawls.

"Oh, ok. There must be a reason for that Marta, these children are lovely. They wouldn't be nasty to you. What did you do?" I gently enquire.

"I didn't do nothing'. Not nothing, not even kicking!" she sobs.

"Kicking?" I probe, seeing a small group of girls approach from a distance, forming a circle around a tiny black and white puppy, taking it in turns to cuddle and love him. One of the teenage girls approaches and smiles, introducing herself as' Sumatiri' and I ask her to explain what happened. She walks slowly towards Marta and takes her hands asking, "Shall I explain or will you?"

Marta hangs her head shamefully and shakes her hands free from Sumatiri's. I urge the young girl to give an account of the incident, but she says that it is important for Marta to relate the story, truthfully, as that way she will not be telling tales or reporting negative incidents. I ask Sumatiri to invite the other children over, with the puppy, so we can sit down and chat. When we are all seated under the shade of a palm tree, I ask Marta to tell me what happened, in front of everyone, so that they can judge the truth of her statement.

"Well Momalu, I is playin' with that girl there," she points to a sweet girl about the same age.

"Ponchella." the girl says.

"Yeh, Ponchella an' the others come in with that little puppy dog..."

"Barney!" Ponchella speaks up again.

"Yeh, Barney an' I runs to pick him up an' he runs away an... an..."

"And what?" I enquire.

Another older girl, about fifteen years of age called Itirka asks, "Why did he run away from you Marta?"

"I dunno, he don't like me!" she replies awkwardly.

"No because you bound up to him roughly and demanded his attention and scooped him up by his tail. He is only a baby. He only knows gentleness and love."

I understand immediately that Marta's background has never shown her gentleness or love, so how could she be expected to be loving and gentle?

"If you want someone to love you, you have to earn their love. You have to show them love and respect them." Itirka says wisely.

"But what did you do to him Marta?" urges Sumatiri.

"I didn't do no nothing!" storms Marta stamping her feet and flailing her arms.

All the children click their tongues and shake their heads disapprovingly and Marta bursts into tears.

"When he ran away from her she followed him into a corner and kicked him!" testifies Ponchella who also bursts into tears along with a few of the other little girls.

"Oh dear! Oh no! Please don't cry!" I utter, dismayed at the information. I understand Marta's behaviour because at the compound all she ever received was abuse and bullying from others.

"We have to make this right! How do we do this Sumatiri?"

"Well she must say sorry to all of us and then she must say sorry to Barney and she must love him and kiss him and then she must spend a day appreciating the beauty of nature."

I nod, thinking it's quite a lot of penitence for one little girl, but I agree and watch Marta apologise to each child as they kiss her on the cheek in return. Then she crouches in the sand and approaches Barney, who has forgiven her and is ready for a game, leaping and bounding around jumping all over her and licking her face, which Marta loves.

"See Momalu, he loves me!"

Tears well as I watch her squeal with delight at the puppy's antics and see all the children joining in, laughing and rolling around in the sand.

"You see Marta, if you show him love, he will love you too!" laughs Sumatiri.

The children run around with Barney, laughing and playing catch- ball and I marvel how quickly they have mended the rift between them. I can't help wishing that it was as easy to mend wars back on earth.

"Now she must go to the flower garden to spend time with the beautiful flowers," states Sumatiri. Agreeing, I offer to go with her, but Sumatiri says I can walk with her to the garden but Marta must stay there alone. Matu the gardener will show her what to do.

I am apprehensive about leaving her, like a mum leaving her child on the first day at school, but I acquiesce to the tribal law. I kiss Marta goodbye and watch her little legs walk slowly up the hill to the glorious flower enclosure. I know she will learn a valuable lesson for her future role and although she will return back to earth as a new-born baby, memory cells within her DNA structure will provide a bank of knowledge that she will be able to access.

Walking back along the sea-shore I spy the men returning from their successful fishing trip and watch them unload the shining, silver fish that leap and jump in the nets in the bright sunshine. Ji helps them to untangle the catch and prepare the fish for the women to cook. I think about the division of labour amongst these people with their strong sense of male and female roles and accept their philosophy that men have certain tasks to perform because of their physical strength. However, apart from the physical aspects of their roles, both men and women enjoy the freedom of just being themselves. Love has no boundaries in this dimension and life is considered a most precious gift. I ask Myaka about old age and death and she explains;

"Growing old is a matter of choice. Take the Chief, he has chosen to grow old and die when it is his time. Others stay at a chosen age for as long as they wish and others place their life in the hands of destiny and lead life to its natural course. It is different for everyone. Existence is a choice, life is an endowment to be treasured and we can, if we want, experience eternal reality."

I am surprised at the idea of 'eternal reality' but in such a beautiful, idyllic paradise, I too might consider the thought of a forever existence in a heavenly utopia.

The day rolls lazily into itself and Ji and I take the opportunity to be with each other and share a wonderful harmonious space, free from any burdens or worries. Towards the end of the afternoon, it is time to collect Marta and I am curious to know what she has learnt. I am allowed inside the garden enclosure and Matu nods and points me in the direction where Marta is busy dusting black roses. She smiles when she sees me but carries on dusting the particles of sand which have blown across from the beach and are embedded in the rose's dark petals.

"You see Momalu, these is precious roses. They is special because there is not many black roses. They is my favourite and when I finish Matu says I can pick one for myself!"

"Ooh, that is lovely," I smile at her dedication to the task.

I watch her tenderly dust the petals. No sooner has she cleared one rose than the sand particles blow back on the wind. I point out to her that her job is very difficult, keeping the roses clean and she replies:

"Yes, Matu says it ain't a useless job, 'cos for a few minutes the rose knows what it's like to be free of the dirt, see? So I keeps doin' it!"

Matu appears smiling, praising Marta for her wonderful work and he asks her to choose a special black rose. She stands up and dusts down her apron and takes a good long look at all of them and declares:
"I don't know which one to choose, 'cos they is all the same!"

Matu laughs and places his hand on her shoulder and asks her which one was the most difficult to clean. She immediately points to a rose in full bloom stating,

"This one, it has so many petals! I gets angry with it an' I spits on it like this!" She demonstrates spitting into the petals and scraping off the beads of sand," an' then I is too rough with the petals an' one gets squashed and then I is sorry, so I do it better an' I knows it likes me, 'cos I got it clean."

"So that's the one for you little lady because you made it yours by taking extra care of it!" he exclaims.

Marta clasps her hands excitedly and watches closely as Matu gently cuts the bloom. She snatches it enthusiastically and a thorn pricks her finger.

"Ouch the damn thing bit me!" she exclaims sucking her bleeding finger.

"Well you see, Marta, most beautiful things in life have their own, natural protection. The rose has thorns, cats have claws and doggies have teeth, so you need to treat them with respect then they will respect you." Matu takes a large leaf and wraps it around her finger and hands back the rose. This time she takes it gently asking;

"What is espect?"

"Respect!" I interject, "Respect means being good to each other and treating people like you want to be treated.

"That's respect!" affirms Matu with a smile as he waves farewell to the group of children excitedly returning to see Marta, greeting her with kisses and hugs. Sumatiri stands in front of her holding a sleepy bundle of fluff which she places gently in Marta's arms saying,

"Now that you know how to treat little ones in your care, you can take care of Barney for a while."

Marta's face lights up, and she beams, exclaiming," Can I? Can I really?"

All the children laugh and trundle off with Marta in the middle holding Barney.

Later that evening in our little hut I peep in to see Marta quietly talking to Barney, who is lying on her chest. As she gently strokes his little nose she says, "I love you Barney, an' I knows you love me too. Ain't that nice? We can be friends forever."

I step back into the shadows, wondering how I am going to separate the two when the time comes. I know it will break Marta's heart to leave Barney. I sigh, thinking that parenting is far more difficult than I ever anticipated. From behind, a hand touches my shoulder and Ji suggests we take a walk up the cliff to watch the moonlight over the sea. In the community, there is no need for babysitters as everyone takes care of everyone else's children, so it is safe to leave Marta playing with Barney for a while. As we climb the steep rocks, Ji's strong hand grips mine, pulling me up some sharp inclines, and I feel the power of his caring protection within me. He has saved Marta and me from unknown horrors, guiding us here to this divine haven and his caring commitment encompasses me in a way I have not dared to imagine. The days we have spent together have been wonderful, growing closer in our peaceful paradise and I have to remind myself that soon I will have to leave, terminating my mission. I realise that if we returned to earth together, my true identity and age would be revealed, so I try not to think about it and indulge my fantasy, enjoying Ji's company too much. Perhaps I love his watchfulness more than anything, as my worries fade when we are together and I have come to rely on him to take care of us. But I have also let him into my heart which I know is a mistake.

I look down at the rocky cliffs and see how far we have climbed in a short time. I hear the waves crash below in the dark and it seems we have been a team forever. It seems a lifetime ago since he first rescued us in the forest. Now the sea is calm and the hypnotic pulse of the waves beat a restful rhythm under the gaze of the full moon, shrouding the clouds in a silver halo. The stars are a diamond-studded blanket in a deep blue canopy, quiet and still. Suddenly, a shooting gem explodes across the cosmos and we follow its pathway into oblivion, where after such a spectacular journey it disintegrates, disappearing without a hint of its former greatness. I heave a sad sigh into the cool night air, sensing a strained distance between us. We are silent, lost in our own thoughts until Ji speaks:

"There is something I have to tell you," he whispers, clutching my hand to his chest." Tonight I must leave!"

His words, the words I have been dreading, are being spoken. I hear them but I don't want to take in their meaning. I don't want to face the next stage of my mission. I don't want to be without him.

"Look, I know this is difficult, but I need you to know the truth," he declares solemnly.

I look into his eyes, puzzled.

"I have to go because your people are coming for you tomorrow and they will come for me... you see I am not on your side," he states coldly.

I don't understand what he is implying and I quickly withdraw my hand from his. I shudder as a cool breeze rides across the beach and darkness descends as the moon plays hide and seek among the ominous clouds. Suddenly I am insecure again, feeling foolish as my bridge to everywhere collapses and I face the stark reality of my reckless emotions.

"I was sent to guide you to Mari and Olav because that was the plan. Someone else was supposed to meet you, but I made sure I got to you first. My orders were to take you to their meeting point, but when I saw you and Marta huddled together, stranded in the forest, I thought of my wife and little son, killed in their quest for freedom and I couldn't do it! I just couldn't hand you over. You reached into my heart and crashed down all the barriers. I was not prepared for that. As a trained soldier I should never allow feelings to interfere with my duty, but I did! I just couldn't endanger your lives, so I took you to a safe place at the farmstead where I decided to give you some training in case we had to face the worst. I had forgotten what it was like to be a real, whole person, feeling important to someone again. You and Marta showed me what I had lost and I couldn't give it up."

"But you killed Mari and Olav and the soldiers? How could you do that?" I ask.

"My need to love, care for and protect the innocent is greater than my obligation to obey orders- I am a soldier, trained to kill and it was their lives or yours!" he replies, turning towards the black sea.

The silence between us is deafening. Somehow I feel cheated, although I should feel grateful. What did Myaka say about the colour of gratitude? That it is 'pink-' well I don't feel 'pink' in this wakening moment. Tears flow quietly and I try to hide my grief but he pulls me to his chest. I sob, "What about on the boat? What about our relationship? Has it all meant nothing to you?"

"It has meant everything to me. Everything, and you will never know how much you have touched my soul. I will never forget us, always know that!" he whispers.

In a moment of despair, it is difficult to balance dignity with a grateful heart. The consequences of words and deeds are too great and almost insurmountable when a heart breaks and hurt floods all senses. Accepting the truth is always hard.

"Perhaps someday I will find you in the past?" he mutters.

I hug him, desperately wanting to believe his words. I need to have some hope to cling to, but my head tells me that I have a mission to complete and meeting again in the past will be virtually impossible. We hold each other for a while allowing our bodies to say what we cannot express, until Ji places his hands on my shoulders and vows:

"There is a place in our hearts where we can always meet. No one can take that away from us."

I know he is right and slowly we make our way down to the damp, sandy beach. Briefly, the moon highlights a silver causeway towards the no-man's land of tomorrow and we know we have to be strong. I ask Ji what will happen to Marta and me and he explains that we will be airlifted to a high-tech city and dropped in the low-life part where there is a Mafia stronghold that rules and controls the time machine. He looks grave.

"Your return has to be organised this way because the Government cannot recognise your undercover status. You have to be careful. Your agent will be vigilant knowing that my people, your enemy, will be watching out for your appearance and will be on the alert, to kidnap Marta. Don't worry. I will be there. I will deploy them and put them off the scent in time for you to make your escape. Look for me in the crowd. I will make sure you are safe. It's not going to be easy. The process is pretty awful, but necessary."

Through a silver pathway across the ocean a strange white metal submarine, shaped like a rocket rises up from the depths and hovers above the water. A small capsule is released from the top of craft which drifts towards us. Ji kisses me for the last time and I watch him step inside the little dome which automatically glides back to the submarine that swallows the capsule whole. Slowly it submerges into the dark, deep ocean.

Aloneness is an empty shell, cracked open by prevailing circumstance and I know I only have myself to blame for my lack of vigilance in allowing light to illuminate the dark caverns of my heart. I was unprofessional and unprepared for these feelings to override my rational thoughts, impairing my judgement. I tell myself it is a lesson well learnt and yet I can't deny the glowing embers alive and warm in my being. I hate myself for being vulnerable but I can't forget what is profound inside and I dread the lonely walk back to the little hut where emptiness awaits. I miss him! Already I miss him so much. With him I grew to know myself and now I am lost.

A gentle voice in the dark greets me and I burst into tears and sob into Chief Monduata shoulders. He pats my head like a loving parent, consoling me with his wise words:

"All phases in life are temporary. All vibrations are continually in flux, so that one minute my dear, your whole world is broken but before long it is mended again. It is better for the breaking because it is transformed anew and the flaw becomes not an error, but beauty."

"I know you are right and I listen to your wisdom but I am disappointed with myself for letting my guard down and for...."

"Being human?" he interjects." Disappointment entices the predator to steal your self-worth!" he cautions," humans are allowed to make mistakes which are merely diversions on life's highway."

"And I am angry with myself for allowing my ego to rule my head."

"Ah, anger ignites trust to swell like yeast in the pot; do not give it heat to rise, for the dough will only taste bitter and you will eat the bread of anguish and retribution."

"I know! I know!" I cry," but I have lived under his protection and guidance and now I am afraid without him!"

"Call your fear an adventure! It is a new chapter in your life where you take his experience and his essence with you. That is his gift to you."

There is nothing more to say. I know I have to be strong for the next part of my mission, I have to be fearless for Marta's sake and for the bigger picture of our destiny. "You must think yourself lucky to have been rescued by Ji and to have spent time together, for I understand he feels lucky to have known your love."

"Yes, Chief, I do feel lucky to have known his love, for the Universe has blessed me and I am indeed Lucky!"

❖

GOING BACK

Back in our little hut Marta is sleeping with Barney snuggled into her. He squints at me through a beady, black eye, keeping watch as I kiss Marta's forehead. He is so cute with his curly black and white coat and sable patch over each ear. How am I going to separate the two in the morning? I gaze over at Ji's empty bed remembering Myaka's words when I asked her about Ji's role in our operation. She said he was my 'emissary' and that she 'couldn't vouch for him'. I now suspect, she knew he was deceitful in his mission, but for the right reasons, for he has a kind, loving heart, wanting only to protect us. I gather up the few things we have accumulated and somehow I regain my composure, as a new strength of purpose guides my actions, recalling the Chief's teaching:-"*Inner peace arises when you choose not to allow another intent, or person or event to control your emotions. You must take sole charge of who you are, what you want to be and where you intend to go. That is the secret to leading a peaceful life.*"

I am not asking for a peaceful life, as I know the next part is going to be tough, but I do ask for inner tranquillity and the strength to carry out my mission effectively. Dawn is about to break and there isn't much time to prepare for leaving and out of the corner of my eye, I spy a strange being in the doorway. Telepathically it communicates with me that we have to leave. The creature is somehow familiar with a large grey head, bulbous black eyes and a small body with long, gangly arms and three fingers on each grey hand. He says he's from Zeta Reticuli and his task is to deliver Marta and me to our destination. He wishes us to hurry as we are to be transported in their craft by interstellar vibration energy which peaks just before dawn. I hand him our bags. With a small, silver device he teleports them to the waiting ship. I wake Marta who is too sleepy to stand and as I try to pick her up the Alien intervenes and extends both his hands. Marta levitates above her bed for a few moments and then vanishes. Myaka appears at the door to say goodbye and scoops up Barney in her arms to take him back to the children. She kisses me and scurries out of the hut. The Alien nods and extends his hands towards me and within a second I am sitting next to Marta in the spaceship. On the outside, the silver craft appears small, but inside when a plasma film seals the door, the interior alters and expands into many sections. Everywhere is a metallic black that changes colour when you move your head and has a shimmering surface afterglow, as though the walls are a mirage. I watch as a being walks through the glowing walls to take a seat in front of us where there are no panels, switches or dials, as the Alien is telepathically wired to the controls and flies the ship purely through his thoughts.

I am relieved that Marta sleeps through the disruption as I know she would be distraught to leave Barney. All is calm aboard the craft as we take off and within a few minutes, we touch down in a deserted area close to a high-tech cityscape. Marta stirs as the craft's interior shrinks, the door evaporates and an alien steps forward to teleport her to a waiting air bus where she falls asleep again. I think the alien has sedated her and I thank him, when I am also teleported to the vehicle, where a stocky, middle-aged woman driver hails us. She is dressed in peculiar Punk attire and has black tattoo designs over her face and neck.

"Hiya, sweetheart! Hop in the love train and tell us your name!" she laughs as we zoom out of sight across the sky through cloud cities and down into the skyscraper, early morning mayhem. She says her name is Polykita but we can call her Polly and explains that she is taking us to a downtown hide-out. The atmosphere changes from the beautiful, serene oasis beyond Earth's ether to a dark, dismal third and fourth density where depressive malignance hangs in the air, like micro shale in a dusty coal field. I shiver, sensing danger ahead. Polly is an excellent driver zig-zagging in and out of flying buses, bikes and hovercrafts until she makes a final kamikaze dive towards a bridge. I close my eyes in horror as she heads straight towards the river. Squinting, through my hands I hold my breath as she swoops under the bridge into a dark safe hold.

"Whoop! Whoop!" shouts Polly as we land safely inside a dingy underground alley, where the stench of sewers wafts through the city tunnels.

"All out, everybody shout, let's get together, you're light as a feather..." she sings as she lifts Marta out of the airbus and into a broken-down lift. I follow with our bags, feeling uneasy in the dank, dirty cavern. We rumble to the top floor where Polly carries Marta to a little apartment and lays her carefully on a small, rickety bed.

"There she goes, steady as she blows," chants Polly and I wonder if she is capable of making sensible conversation, but as she turns around I spy at the back of her head, a round chip with little lights flashing on and off. I understand that she is an Android, the kind that mostly communicates in rhyme the product of a faulty batch that the engineers did not manage to recall in full. Ji had told me about them when he explained the cyber world and said many mistakes had been made with some of the Android batches. Apparently, some were argumentative and overly aggressive, some were deliberately disobedient, some were destructive instead of being helpful. The manufacturers had difficulty in tracking down all the faulty ones, so there were still flawed machines in use, which perfectly explained Polly, still going strong, a benevolent rhyming machine.

"Well hello there!" croons a colourful lady in a red Charleston frock and feather boa trailing over her shoulders, holding a long empty cigarette holder, on which she occasionally sucks, as she poses dramatically against the door. Her curly, red hair is held in place with a pink bandana and a pink feather pokes out from the top of her head, like a caricature of Pocahontas. Her bright red lipstick gleams in the gloom as she taps her black patent shoes on the hard floor, as though she is about to partner Fred Astaire in a ballroom fantasy dance. I can't believe I have been transported to such a dismal place with such strange, eccentric people, but I accept my fate, graciously.

"I'll be back, quick as a hat!" chants Polly as she exits the bedroom.

"Don't mind Polly, she's a real sweetie, the Southern Belle says in a deep southern drawl. I'm Chantelle by the way and don't worry, you won't have to suffer this hellhole for long, we hope to get you out tomorrow evening, all being well."

I sit on the end of the bed and stroke Marta's head. She is going to be very confused when she wakes. Suddenly Chantelle shouts orders to someone downstairs her southern drawl replaced by a very harsh, gruff masculine voice and I understand she is actually a he. Marta stirs and begins to wake, sitting up and rubbing her eyes as she takes in the strange, new scene. She looks around and then howls and screams, demanding Barney.

"Oooh, such tantrums little lady" croons Chantelle sarcastically, "we can't have that now, can we, disturbing everyone?" Swooping Marta off the bed in his strong arms, he whisks her out of the door and in a panic I follow but somehow he manages to calm her temper tantrum. I spy further down the hallway, in the kitchen, a little boy with a kitten and I gather they are the reason for Marta's mood change. Chantelle introduces Marta to Colin and the two become engrossed in the little ginger kitten, stroking and teasing it with a ribbon on a stick.

"Don't worry, the cat is a cyber and so is Colin!" shouts Chantelle as he enters a closed door. I walk towards the two children playing with the kitten listening to their conversation.

"Every pet should have a name!" insists Marta, "I had a puppy called Barney..." she mumbles as she fights back the tears.

"That's a stupid name!" Colin retorts.

"No it aint!" shouts Marta, stamping her feet.

"Tis so!" screams Colin as he pushes Marta and she retaliates by pushing him back and suddenly, the two are rolling around on the kitchen floor, kicking, biting and punching. Chantelle's door flings open and a large commanding army officer strides towards the children and separates them, picking each up by the scruff of the neck, bellowing a warning to them both to be quiet and stop fighting.

"He started it!" chunters Marta, under her breath.

I glare at Marta and she sits down quietly at the table opposite Colin. Meanwhile, the kitten has switched itself off in the fracas. "Now look what you've done, we'll have to switch him back on again!" states Colin authoritatively.

"I still think he should have a name," insists Marta, "you could call him Ginger, 'cos he is ginger colour!"

"That's stupid!" retorts Colin.

"Why?" questions Marta.

"Well, you're not called Blackie, because you've got black hair!"

Marta's hair, since it was shaved initially, has grown into beautiful, little ringlets and she looks lovely. In the heat of the paradise island, the children persuaded her to abandon her pink bobble hat replacing it with pretty pink hibiscus flowers. "I don't care if he doesn't have a name then!" Marta says scornfully.

"He has a name, dummy!" Colin chides.

I can't help thinking it's a bit rich for Colin to call Marta a 'dummy' given the fact that he is an Android.

"Yeh, what is it then?" screams Marta.

"Kitten, he likes to be called Kitten!" Colin adds pointedly as he switches the cybercat back on.

"Sorry, he is so argumentative." The Commander says. "We ordered a nice young boy as our family front, but he has a malfunction, so he'll have to go back. Perhaps they can replace him with a nice, sweet little girl," the Commander smiles. He looks vaguely familiar as he places a pile of old-fashioned children's books on the table for the children.

"We kept these hidden from the Literature Controllers." He says. "Such a shame to have all books destroyed. There's nothing quite like the feel of a book and the anticipation of physically turning over the pages, don't you think?"

I nod, feeling sad that the new world is so high-tech, controlled only through internet communication. The Commander sits next to the children pouring nostalgically over illustrations of animals and insects. Marta points to a scary picture of a large black spider asking him what kind of creature it is. The Commander explains it is an insect which is extinct in the New World Order which had cleaned the planet of animals and creatures that were extraneous to high-tech living." You can, of course, get cyber replicas of certain creatures if you want," explains the Commander.

"What does this spider critter eat for dinner?" asks Marta inspecting the picture closely.

"Well spiders used to eat smaller insects, like flies," adds the Commander.

"And what does they have for their pudding?" enquires Marta, seriously.

I try not to laugh but argumentative Colin is ready. "They didn't have pudding, dummy!

"Well we did on the island every day. We has fruit and all kinds of sweet things. Anyway they critters don't not eat anyfin' anymore 'cos they not around 'cos they stink!" argues Marta.

The Commander laughs and I correct Marta, "extinct, darling! Extinct!"

Colin scorns Marta and they begin to fight again.

"That's it, no more! You're going back Colin!" shouts the Commander impatiently as he switches him off.

Marta looks horrified and becomes very subdued as the boy Colin fades from his animated cyborg- self into a doll-like, plastic machine. The Commander wheels him away, putting him into a cupboard and carries the floppy, dead cyber kitten to its resting place in a drawer. Marta has never encountered cybers and she is shocked that they're not real. She holds my hand and whispers in my ear: "Is I real, Momalu?"

"Of course you are real darling. In this strange world, you never know now who is real and who isn't. I'm afraid it's just the way things are, so we have to be careful who we trust, all the time. Understand?"

She nods and says," I is hungry Momalu!"

The Commander hears her and jumps into action saying," Oh I'm sorry, I'm not being a very good host - or hostess!" He says the last words in Chantelle's Southern drawl and I gasp in recognition of his disguise. "Ah yes, now you get it dear. We have to be a master of disguise around here. Do you both like Baluga bolga?"

Marta and I look at each other not recognising the dish but we are both so hungry that we are prepared to try almost anything. It turns out to be a chemical mixture representing pizza, spaghetti bolognaise and a beef burger which Marta and I eat, finding it reasonably tasty, after which the Commander shows us to a tiny bedroom where we both, almost instantaneously, fall asleep.

In the morning the Commander wakes us, dressed as a cleaning lady complete with a neat grey uniform and short black wig. He introduces us to his new little cyber girl, who is slightly older than Marta and is called Stephanie. She seems sweet and placid and helps Marta with the breakfast cereals. The Commander explains that he has to set things up for the evening and we will be taken to the teleportation transit compound when it is safe. In the meantime we can relax and play games with Stephanie. The Commander disappears with a mechanised mop and brush to complete his disguise and says goodbye in a strange accent. As the day wears on I feel obliged to explain to Marta what is about to happen to us and I take her to a quiet corner to prepare her saying, "you do want to have a wonderful Mum and Dad who will love you and look after you and give you the very best of everything, don't you?"

"I don't need no one else, I got you Momalu!" she exclaims.

"Yes, but darling, we talked about this before, we are going to take a very important trip back home to meet your Mum and Dad who are waiting for you."

"Is they real?" she enquires.

"Of course they are real and they love you so much."

"But, I want you to come too, Momalu," she cries.

"Look, I will be with you always, in here and in here," I whisper pointing to her heart and head. "Do you remember the special black rose that you chose?"

She nods with tears streaming down her face. "You chose it because you took care of it the most and it needed you the most and so you loved it the most, remember?"

"Yes Momalu. Do you like black roses too?"

"Yes, but my favourite roses are yellow climbing roses, they smell so sweet and look so bright and happy and they climb over garden walls and fences and nothing stops them," I reply nostalgically.

"I like yellow roses too, but the black ones are best, 'cos the gardener said they is for power and strength," I smile as she demonstrates power with clenched fists.

"Well tonight, I want you to think about your black rose and be as strong and powerful as that lovely flower because we are going on an adventure, won't that be fun? "

Marta stands to attention like Ji taught her and salutes. I laugh at her antics. She is such a character!

Later, in the afternoon the Commander returns and while Stephanie and Marta are playing cyber games, he calls me into his office, explaining that everything is set for our departure. We have to leave at twilight as it is the time when the carnival begins and we are to be disguised as fiesta performers. I thought Marta would enjoy that as it would distract her from the anguish of our separation.

"You'll see I think you will look good as a ballerina! He smiles, "Here try this costume and wig and there's a fiesta mask for you, too." He makes the art of disguise look so easy and I compliment him on his choice and he responds with:

"You see my dear, the art of disguise must appear effortless but the illusion of being effortless requires a great deal of effort and background preparation. Believe me I am a genius in this field. This evening I will be Cocoa the Clown. Voila!" He points to a full clown costume hanging by the closet.

"What is Marta going to be?" I enquire curiously.

"Ahh the piece de resistance!" he laughs gleefully clapping his hands and holding up a penguin costume!"

I am a little shocked and wonder whether she will like it but the Commander seems to think Marta will love it. He calls her into the office and shows her the outfit. She looks at it curiously but she doesn't know what a penguin is, so the Commander shows her a picture of a penguin explaining that it used to live in a very cold place with Polar bears.

"Oh I knows all about Polar bears, don't I Momalu? They got black skin like me. Can't I be a Polar bear?" she whines.

The Commander looks a little disappointed, sighs and reluctantly fumbles inside a large walk-in wardrobe and produces a dusty little Polar bear all-in-one costume. Marta is delighted and can't wait to try it on. When we have the head fixed, she looks just like a baby Polar bear jumping up and down in front of the mirror. Wearing the head is a little hot for her but the Commander explains that she won't be a real Polar bear if she doesn't wear the head. When we are all dressed in our costumes and the Commander and I are fully made up, we slip outside into a nightmare, mayhem of fairground cacophony, market-place pandemonium and zoo-like screeching from a multitude of costumed animals. The Carnival has begun and the masses are already hyped into a frenzied, hysterical broth of drunken, drugged anarchy. I cling onto my little bewildered Polar bear and Cocoa the clown laughs his way mockingly through the chaos, leading the way across the riotous mob.

The night is electrically fired with neon glare and sexual provocation on every street. Buildings in the shape of naked women flaunt and taunt the punters with their erotic displays and the air is tainted with the smell of alcohol, sour marijuana and cheap perfume. Among the costumed disarray of party-goers, strange half-broken androids wander aimlessly along the sidewalks with sparking electronics buzzing from their mouths and ears. Abandoned cyborgs and robots lie heaped in shop doorways ready to be collected with tomorrow's garbage. In the town square a large wire cage imprisons hybrid aliens, hybrid humans and animal creatures brought out for the night's cruel killing games. I am overwhelmed and shocked to be embroiled in the night's horrific entertainment, especially after the beautiful island paradise we have just left and also knowing that farther up in the cityscape, life is so clinically clean and different where hi-tech existence in a cold, detached structure, void of inessential emotion, is deemed to be the zenith of modern living.

Out of the corner of my eye I detect a shadow following us. I turn to see who it is but see only the shadows from the mob, dancing and spiralling on the sidewalk. The Commander quickly ushers us over a bridge, where for a few moments the crowd pins us against the wall and I have to grip Marta's hand very hard. Suddenly Marta's hand is wrenched from me and try as I might, I can't budge to get to her. The strange black shadow is close and I sense it retrieve Marta's hand and place it back in mine. I can't move my head to look, I only sense the protective presence. When the mass surges forward and we are released, I search the throng for the invisible angel, but our benefactor has disappeared.

The Commander leads us down some dark alleyways and through a disused hospital. I'm still conscious of someone ghosting our moves. I see a person dressed as a skeleton wearing a top hat but I think my mind must be playing tricks in the heat of the night. At the back of the empty hospital is a disused car park and hastily we make for a flight of concrete steps leading into the dark bowels of the garage. I peep behind us and catch a glimpse of the skeleton tracking us and I am afraid. Down and down we race into the darkness. Marta's little legs can't carry her so fast and she stops. I whip off her Polar bear head to allow her to breathe. Her little head is wet with sweat and her face is dripping. She is gasping for air and crying at the same time. The Commander has disappeared into the depths and I begin to shake as I wipe Marta's head and face with my ballerina skirt. I don't know what to do or where to go. Marta is distressed and unable to move. She is too heavy for me to carry and I can't see the steps in the dark without the Commander leading us. Marta begins to howl as she regains her breath and her voice echoes down the tunnel in a scary reveille, like a bugle call at dawn. I try to hush her and soothe her fears but she is terrified and so am I. My heart is pounding and I want to faint. Suddenly out of the shadows, the skeleton jumps down and I leap in front of Marta. The skeleton places a plastic false hand over my mouth and puts his arm gently around my waist. My body sinks into his and I know his touch. Ji is our angel, our saviour, as he promised he would be. Marta stops crying and whispers:

"Ji, why is you a skeleton?"

He doesn't reply but hugs her and we all huddle together for a few moments. The Commander, racing back up the stairs is angry that we lost him and is shocked to see Ji, but relieved that we are not in the hands of the enemy. He tells us to follow him closely. Eventually, we drop onto a disused railway line and follow that into a large tunnel where lights are blazing and the faint sound of voices float through a dilapidated brick wall where we join a long queue and shed some of our costumes. Officials hand out long, white linen gowns, like hospital operating smocks, to everyone in the queue and we are told to leave our own clothes on the floor and put on the gowns. The Commander takes off his clown wig and suit revealing a black uniform like the officials in charge of the complex are wearing. I look behind to smile at Ji, but he has disappeared. Marta is happy to take off her Polar bear suit and is more comfortable in the free-flowing gown as cold air sweeps through the tunnels and we are relieved to be free from the night brawlers.

The waiting travellers are subdued, perhaps apprehensive of the journey and a few people ahead of us are carrying babies. I look down at Marta and sigh. My heart is breaking and my head is in turmoil. I am so glad she is unaware that we will never see each other again and I hug her as she presses her little arms around my legs and buries her head in my thighs.

"We are going on a journey back to meet your wonderful parents who are waiting for you. The transport is a little strange and you have to be brave, like your black rose, ok?" I say with a lump in my throat. "We will stand together on a little platform and I will hold you tight. A funny cage will come over us and we will fly back home." I explain. The words almost choke me and I fight to remain calm. When I accepted the mission I never realised how painful the final parting would be. I tell myself, I never realised the depth of love I would give and receive in return.

"Momalu, I am hungry!" states Marta and I laugh because it's the first time she has said, 'I am!' instead of 'I is'.

The Commander leaves us for a few minutes and returns with water and candy for Marta. The line moves slowly until we enter a type of arena where the officials are checking all the gowned travellers. The families of the travellers leave the queue to watch the departure from the auditorium. As we near the podium I am alarmed to see people treated like cattle, shunted along to the wire cage with black prodding sticks. Haunted eyes stare blankly as the death trap descends, shrouding the travellers in a purple, smoky haze. Some are successful and some are not. I don't allow Marta to see the mess left by the trapped travellers who do not survive the process, their melted charred flesh is soon cleaned and cleared by the express cleaners.

"It's what you get for taking risks with the Mafia!" I hear one man mutter, as another body disintegrates in the purple haze. As we near the stand I spy Ji in the crowd watching us, protectively. Now it is our turn next and the Commander escorts us to the cage, preventing the officials from poking us with their black truncheons. Just as we are about to step inside the cage, an official steps forward and my heart sinks. The Commander chats with him for a few moments and Ji moves forwards in preparation to take action in case anything goes wrong. The Commander reassures the official that all is in order and Ji steps back.

Standing in our flimsy gowns with the wind whistling though the arena I feel helpless and vulnerable as little Marta clings to my legs and I hold on to her tightly. I thank the Commander for all his help and he smiles saying,

"Remember there is no such thing as failure-it's just success waiting to take its turn!"

I look into the crowd to see Ji for the last time and we exchange a loving look. I hear Marta singing her favourite song as the cage descends:

"The sun will come out tomorrow, bet your bottom dollar, that tomorrow there'll be sun..."

The purple hazy smoke engulfs us and all I am and all she becomes in the moment of disintegration is all-embracing, powerful 'love' as together we merge into the light of a new dawning and I know I am Lucky, beyond reckoning.

TOMORROW AND TOMORROW AND...

"Tomorrow, tomorrow, I love ya tomorrow..."

The song goes round and round in my head as I gain consciousness back in the past in a familiar hospital bed. Mr Alexander, together with a nurse, stands by my side. They greet me with a smile when I open my eyes.

"Well, well, my dear- congratulations, you made it!" laughs Mr Alexander, grinning with his Chimpanzee smile.

I attempt to sit up but I am told by the nurse to rest for a while.

"Marta? Marta? Where is she?" I whisper, in panic.

"Now don't you worry about her, she is fine and doing well in the nursery. You can see her in a short while, if you like?" soothes Mr Alexander, waving his large hairy hands in the air.

I nod and close my eyes, happy to know that the mission has been successful and relieved that Marta is safe. It is strange being back in the past and I begin to remember everything. I remember it all. I remember the past and the future. I begin to recall details, all wrapped up in a microcosm of a single memory cell. I am ecstatic, knowing that I have lost nothing. I hear the nurse shuffling around my bed and I sit up suddenly saying,

"But I remember everything. I remember it all. How is that possible?"

The nurse laughs and points to the little scar on my right wrist explaining :"see this? Do you remember being bitten by a mosquito before you came here?"

For a moment I search my memory and suddenly it all comes flooding back as she adds, "when it bit you, that little menace of a mosquito passed on its DNA in your blood and we were able to extract your memory cells from him and replace them in your memory bank."

"That's amazing!" I exclaim, mentally thanking the mosquito, although I recall it was a nasty large, infected bite that I must have got on my quarry walk. I wasn't pleased at the time but now I am overjoyed to be able to remember everything. It is odd how little annoying things can turn out to be life-saving in the end. The Nurse helps me out of bed and takes me to the New- Born Nursery. Through the glass window I spy rows of little Perspex pods with tiny babies of all shapes and sizes, all uniformly swathed in white shawls. I immediately spy Marta and a lump forms in my throat. Of course she isn't Marta anymore for her name will change, and her life will unfold and bloom like her black rose, but deep in her psyche she will have stored some of our love and life together.

I stand by her cot. Tears well and I can't believe my truculent little girl is so beautiful, so tiny and perfect. In my head I hear her little voice calling - "Momalu, I is hungry!"

"May I hold her?" I ask the nurse tentatively and she nods, helping me snuggle the little warm bundle into my arms. The surge of love, the well of delight is unimaginable. To hold her again is bliss beyond belief! I uncover her teeny hands, noting nature's perfection in miniature, the beautiful little nails. I recall the horrific state in which I first found her and all the traumatic 'firsts' we went through together and how she learnt everything so quickly with her great thirst for knowledge. I will never forget her. Looking into her sweet baby face, I softly sing her favourite song- 'the sun will come out tomorrow' and she opens her big eyes wide, as if to say, "what you doing Momalu, I is trying to get to sleep?" The nurse gently takes her, explaining that her parents have arrived. I hand her back and watch from a distance as a lovely young couple enter the nursery. Her mother-to-be is blonde, beautiful, and looks kind and gentle, and her father-to-be is an athletic black man, full of pride and love as he takes his new baby daughter in his arms. I imagine the couple to be similar to Marta's first genetic parents. My heart aches as they leave and I am glad to have stored the memories of our time together. Lost in my journey with Marta, I am surprised when a kind hand pats my shoulder and Mr Alexander, with a sympathetic gesture, leads me back to his office saying he has something to show me and asks me to take a seat at his desk.

"You have done a great job, little lady! We now have everything in place to begin the preparation for great leadership for the future and to take you back to where you belong."

I nod, accepting his compliment.

"But before you go I want to show you something that I think will interest you," he states flicking a switch which dims the lights as a 3D holographic screen slides out from the back wall. A film plays of a beautiful black woman making her inaugural, Presidential speech. Spellbound, I watch as she holds the masses with her brilliant rhetoric. Her gaze is strong and confident and her demeanour graceful and elegant.

"This is her future. She makes a darn good President! You did a good job!" he exclaims.

I am so proud of her and quietly in the back of my mind I hear a sweet little voice asking, 'Momalu, is I real?' Gone is the petulant little, lovable girl and in her place stands a powerful, magnificent woman. I sigh, she really is amazing! Does she marry and have children of her own?" I enquire.

"No, no, she never gets married as she is really dedicated to her political career, but she does have two passions. One of her delights is watching Musicals and I believe her favourite is 'Annie' and the other love is gardening. She has a great affiliation, apparently, for roses and actually creates a new hybrid rose with an unusual combination of colours - it's a black rose with yellow trim petals that she calls 'Momalu'. Strange name, but I guess it means something to her!"

Mr Alexander leaves me alone to gather my thoughts. Somewhere, somehow, my lovely girl has hidden recollections of us both, stored in her computer brain and the love we shared will be a warm reminiscence embedded in her soul. Maybe someday, somewhere in the cosmos we will meet again?

All things pure and good in this Universe are never lost; only nothing remains nothing but everything is everything in the Great Universal Primal Spark of eternity. A nurse enters and disturbs my thoughts.

I take a last glance at the magnificent lady President's frozen picture on the screen as I say a final goodbye to Marta. The Nurse leads me to the Teletransportation Centre where I am to be teleported back to my original timeline and I am confident that I will find myself again, where I left myself back in another past.

And there you have it Rosie – that was my amazing and incredible journey to the future to bring back the first black, lady President. Of course no one will believe it, but when it transpires, they will think twice about the 'truth', like the time I predicted the Pandemic eight years before it happened. Do you remember Rosie?

"Brought you a nice cup of tea Rosie," smiles Estrella, "how's it all going?"

"Well, I've nearly finished 'Lucky 2 Love' but I've got a strange feeling, she's got another surprise for me!" laughs Rosie.

"Yes, if there's one thing you can count on and that is she is always predictably unpredictable!" Both women laugh as Rosie is left to drink her tea and ponder the next file waiting to be explored. She sighs as she reads the final pages of 'Lucky 2 Love'

Well Rosie,

I am sure you have done a grand job of sifting through all my notes about Marta. I have to say it was a very challenging mission and yet one of the most rewarding. Do you recall when an elderly Korean, ex-soldier came to visit me? Well here is my account, you may find it interesting?

The return teleportation was easy. I lay down in the machine and within seconds was back. My youthful body is elderly again with wrinkled hands and worn-out legs and as I step back into my lost past, which is now my present, I am grateful to remember everything. In my office in the Sanctuary, I look at the photographs of my children, grandchildren and great grandchildren and I am thankful to the Universe for allowing me the extravagance of living a full and wondrous life. Travelling to and fro through timelines, I realise that the only sustaining element of life is 'love' and I am always reminded of my Tibetan monk friend and mentor- Yuli teaching me about 'love':

"Love is bestowed for the power of energetic exchange between the loved and the love one. The moment you become 'love' itself, is the moment you stop being a slave, for true love is a weapon like no other. It is a complete code of practice and if you are 'love' then you are everything to everyone and all to yourself."

I remember Ji and the brief time we spent together in our beautiful island paradise. He had become my protector by chance, when he should have been my enemy and we blended into each other's souls like the Yin and Yang of the cosmos. We took our moments of sheer joy for granted, not counting the hours to our departing destiny, living only in the moment and for the moment. Perhaps that's how life should be? My thoughts are interrupted by a knock at the door and Estrella breezes in smiling wryly as she announces-

"You have a visitor mum, shall I bring him in?"

I am surprised as I have only just returned from my difficult mission and I enquire who it is but Estrella teases saying, "You'll see!"

I have my back to the door, staring out of the window into the beautiful garden as I hear someone enter shuffling their elderly feet on the polished floor. I hear his voice and I am nervous to turn around. My heart quickens and I am ashamed to appear so old and different from my youthful self, but when I see his aged smile, I am reassured and we clutch each other like old book-ends, afraid to let go in case we both fall.

"I never thought I would see you again," I whisper.

Ji laughs quietly and holds me at arm's length looking directly into my eyes, "I promised I would find you."

I turn away shyly, wondering what he might be thinking seeing my aged face and remembering our happy, youthful days together.

"Look at me?" he says gently, "no, look at me? Do you think a few years make any difference to how I feel about you and always will?"

Tears stream as I snuggle into his chest, "but how did you get here?" I question.

"They allowed me a little window in time to visit you, amplifying my years so that we would be the same," he smiles, "let's sit down, advancing years are not too kind to the body!"

I laugh as we both sit and Estrella bounds in with a tea tray full of afternoon goodies. She chats to Ji as she serves us and is fascinated to learn about our 'Marta' mission and our experiences. She invites Ji to stay the night but he declines as his time slot will soon fade and he will be transferred back to his own timeline. When Estrella leaves, Ji puts down his plate and looks at my photos asking about the grandchildren. He picks up the photo of Craig.

"Craig and I were very close. He passed over a few years ago. He was a wonderful man," I tell him.

Ji nods and puts the photo back on my desk adding: "look, you don't have to stay here, you can come with me and we can be together again!"

But as much as I am tempted, I know I cannot, because apart from not wanting to leave my family, the risks of travelling on his transit timeline might mean losing my own cell structure. Ji understands my concerns and is disappointed, but we both know, deep down, it would not be possible. He puts his arms around me and holds me close whispering:

"There is nothing wrong in connecting to a field of dreams. I can always dream of being with you and maybe sometime in the future our paths will cross; especially if we create an energy space in time and compel our desires to manifest. If a relationship is not about love it won't survive, but I know ours will."

A shimmering glow descends around him separating me from his embrace as he stands alone in a cubicle of light. Energy vibration consumes his body travelling from his feet upwards, until there is nothing left but an afterglow of sunbeams catching the rays of dust in the air.

In the emptiness of the moment there is power that is both gone and yet left behind. Ji was powerful and yet gentle and I am left in awe of his gentleness, like the impact of a snowflake, the last to fall, can cause an avalanche and the strength of a raindrop can both save life and cause floods to destroy it. The gentle glow of a sunbeam nurturing the earth, with its loving warmth, can, with greater intensity burn all that it helped to create and the strength of a breath of air kissing the trees can be soothing, yet in a storm the song of the earth can be shattered by nature's elemental power. Where is my now? I am neither happy nor sad. I know in this moment in time, I just am and for that I am lucky.

⋯•◄❮❯►•⋯

THERE IS NO END – ONLY NEW BEGINNINGS

So Rosie,

You have the complete file of 'Lucky 2 Love' but as you have probably guessed - there is more to come, much more! I have not spoken about the third file as the contents will be outrageous to most people and yet by the time 'Lucky 3 – Knowledge is the Key' is available, much of the information will have been revealed, especially by the American government, who have a legal responsibility to their country to tell the truth about secret documents that have been hidden for decades. The film industry and the media have been preparing people for years to accept impossible and unbelievable facts about Aliens, UFO's, Time Travel, Secret Space Forces, Life on other planets, Intergalactic Warfare and many more surprising truths about the earth's real history and the emergence of humanity.

As I am writing this Rosie, I have in front of me a copy of one of the latest American documents giving unbelievable facts about time travel transit time. You can check these facts on Linda Moulton Howe's Earth file reports, as she is one of our major, brave journalists and reporters in this field. Her books are incredible and will verify astonishing information I have shared with you. The document states that travelling a hundred times faster than the speed of light, from the earth, planet Mars can be reached in one hundred and ninety-three seconds. Jupiter can be reached in thirty-six minutes, Alpha Centauri can be reached in fifteen days and the Orion Nebula can be reached in 1.3 years. Isn't that amazing Rosie?

'Lucky 3 – Knowledge is the Key' reveals many more wondrous, outrageous and incredible events which I have experienced and the purpose of informing everyone is to illuminate and enrich their options so that they can make informed life choices. You see Rosie, making a choice to stand back and view your world, equipped with new knowledge and allowing your imagination to soar into unknown pastures of belief, will expand your consciousness into realms of truth you never knew existed. But first you have to wipe the slate clean of all previous ideas and notions, breaking through any barriers that prevent you from taking a leap into completely new territory. As Dr Wayne Dyer says in 'Wishes Fulfilled', "Don't contaminate your imagination with thoughts of how your life used to be!"

I walk into the garden with the faint floral scent of early morning dew glistening on the yellow roses and purple lavender, feeling at peace. I sit down in my meditation seat, designed for quiet repose and close my eyes. Almost immediately, a male figure appears through a hazy shroud surrounded by an intense turquoise light. His pale face is blurred and his elongated body is cloaked in a long blue robe. Telepathically I am told he is one of the Janos people, a human-like, alien race. It is documented that on June 19, 1978, a family of three adults and two small children were taken on board a Janos spaceship to travel to their planet where they were able to witness the Janos way of life. Separate accounts from the adults and children all verify the same story with accurate details and description of the Janos people, their families, their houses and the planet. I am informed that the word 'Janos' means 'God Gracious, God Merciful' represents 'new beginnings' while the turquoise light brings protection, tranquillity, wisdom, healing energy and everlasting love. I try to bring his face into focus. It remains indistinct but I can clearly hear his voice saying: "It is important to question the very fibre of your existence on Earth, examine minutely why you chose to incarnate on this planet. If you do not find exuberance and joy in your daily existence, then you will remain in a dark shadowland encompassed by lurking fears that will block out the sunshine. Remember, on earth nothing is of nothing but everything is all. If you plant nothing, then nothing you will reap, but if you embrace all in love, then everything is yours. Nothing is trivial when you look from the other side, even the smallest act of love is bountiful."

The turquoise glow fades and I open my eyes to gaze into the sky, wondering where the Janos people live, envying their harmonious existence, reminding myself that planet Earth is a place of learning and spiritual growth and not created for the comfort of perpetual harmony, which means that we must question 'what' and 'who' is really manipulating the world. It is a lie that humans are the only life force in the Universe. I know this to be so from my experiences beyond the possible and now scientists have verified that there are three hundred million habitable planets in our galaxy and they speculate there could be more. NASA has been involved in a massive cover-up programme for many years, involving secret bases on the Moon, Aliens and UFO craft. They have a special department, whose sole purpose is to air-brush out any photographic evidence that reveals the truth about secret information. Whistle-blowers from that department have vouched for the authenticity of the unit's deceitful activities.

From my experience, Rosie, the Moon is not the grey, desolate planet you have been brain-washed into believing it to be, as I know there are regions that are extremely beautiful especially on the far side, where you can breathe unaided in the forests, mountains and by the lakes. Many nations have bases on the Moon and inside are various levels where satellite communication is exchanged throughout the cosmos. Likewise, Mars has been inhabited by many Nations for a long time and I have remote-viewed some terrible things that are happening on Mars. Meanwhile, entrepreneurs, like Elon Musk want to transfer people to Mars to populate the planet with new blood!

Rosie, you have travelled far with me, on many adventures and there are many more to come, but I would like you to ask yourself a series of 'what if' questions, allowing yourself the opportunity to address uncomfortable hypotheses.

What if you discovered that you live in a world of deceit and illusion controlled by others who are not human? Would that discovery, if it were true, affect you and the concept you have of yourself and would it change your life's purpose?

What if I suggested that your life might be viewed as a commodity, enmeshed inside a container by predators who wish to ensnare your energy and consign it to perpetual slavery?

What if the world, our earth is a holographic grid?

What if I were to prove to you that the two world wars were planned in 1871 by Cardinal Mazzini and Albert Pike? The proof is contained in their letters to each other which can be researched and which outline the political tactics, military strategies and the outcome of both wars.

What if the Pope and the British Royal family harbour dark secrets? Do you know that there is a white Pope and a black Pope and both have to agree to the election of American Presidents?

What if the Church of England and the Church of Rome are built on the grey side of evil?

What if the world is ruled from a base in Antarctica by beings who were the first to inhabit the earth and have far superior intelligence and technical knowledge than humans?

These suggestions are alarming to the uninitiated who have not yet delved into the murky undercurrent of the sewers beneath a sterilised existence.

So, you see Rosie, you are going to struggle with the third file and the extreme information that will be disclosed, but I feel it is our duty to enlighten people to the realisation that the world is not the place they believe it is. World History, for example, has been distorted and documented to suit the purpose of the Beings that really rule and have prevented humans from learning about their true lineage.

Our skies are no longer natural and have been tampered with Chemtrails and modified by machines like massive micro-wave ovens shooting electromagnetic vibrations through the ionosphere and manipulating, modifying and controlling the weather. High Frequency Active Auroral Research Programme (**H.A.A.R.P.**) has been created to deliberately alter our climate and environment. In addition it can also alter human awareness and behaviour. When I travelled to China to learn how to be a Panda keeper, because I love Pandas, I learnt that the Chinese Government has a bureau especially dedicated to weather modification and have used their knowledge both today and in the past to control the weather, they did that for the 2008 Olympic Games. Russia has the same technology and has even used their equipment to manipulate the weather to ensure good sunny days for major holidays. In England Paul McCartney spent a tremendous amount of money in modifying the weather to make sure it was a clear sunny day for his London concert in the park. The weather was also modified, so I have been informed, for Harry and Megan's royal wedding. Apparently, there was a fault in the technology on that occasion and the programme was protracted, so not only was it a hot sunny day for the ceremony but the hot weather continued for three weeks afterwards, causing a drought in places and the deaths of some elderly people caused by the heatwave. This is just a taste Rosie, of the shocking information I have stored in the red file.

The world is rapidly changing and one day we will not recognise our earth, as the planet it once was allowed to be and even by the time you read this you will already be hundreds of nanotech steps closer to being farther away from the Homo-Sapien you know yourself to be and hundreds of nanotech steps nearer to becoming post-human. Technological advances are shaping our world and its inhabitants resulting in an almost unrecognisable planet, even from fifty years ago. Brave New World is on the horizon and in many cases is already here. Transhumanism and the opportunity to be a superior human being is on the rise on a global scale and the notion of enforced transhumanism is not too far in the distant future and that is why we must be fully armed with knowledge to make clear choices about our future development.

I know what you are going to say Rosie and yes, of course it is perfectly possible and acceptable to live a life without questioning anything, burying your head in the sand, but you have to ask yourself the question - 'am I living or hiding?' Remember I have seen many aspects of the future that I believe are not in our favour and little by little our human rights are being deceitfully sliced away. I believe that the information in the red file will hopefully entice a healthy curiosity and encourage people to delve into forbidden territory to seek out the truth and to question everything. Once you begin on the pathway to 'truth-seeking' you will never see, hear and accept all that is conventional again. As you demand a higher-conscious awareness of everything, you will seek the same energy goodness in your reality and in doing so, you will unconsciously remove limitations you have placed upon yourself, thus allowing yourself to experience a higher realm of 'limitlessness'.

Where is the 'now'? I am sitting on my decking in my little cabin in a woodland park surrounded by lush trees and vegetation. It is June and my potted plants and flowers blaze brightly against the wild poppies and deep purple rhododendrons nestling in the tall ferns. Wood pigeons continually coo and thrash through the copse opposite, while a tiny Jenny Wren dares to peep through my Buddleia tree and hop teasingly on my wooden railings. A wood-pigeon has nested in the silver birch tree overhanging my decking and two chicks have hatched. I watch them grow daily and I am grateful for nature's diurnal miracle. One day they will learn to fly and I will be glad I was a tiny part of their existence. The breeze sighs gently amongst the Bamboo bushes and the smell of Citronella incense and candles ward off the midges and mosquitoes. I am content in the moment and am grateful to the Universe for the happiness I have known and will have in the future.

In the tranquillity, I close my eyes and drift into a magical kingdom beyond this sphere where Mimi, my golden dragon waits. She chose me as her human Connector and our short journey together so far, has been truly wonderful and enlightening, teaching me many aspects of Dragon Law. She is now mature, so different from the little petulant six-year-old Mimi I first met and our truculent misunderstandings we initially exchanged, belong to the distant past. We are spiritually tied and she holds the secrets of my heart. Her beauty is power and her strength is love and I am awed in the presence of her supreme knowledge. She is pleased to see me and asks :
"Are you happy?"

I am not sure how to reply as I know I am happy, but what is happiness? In the silence Mimi observes me and telepathically offers her wisdom saying:

"Existing in joyous harmony with your surroundings is the highest code of practice that you can achieve but living your life in and

through 'joy' is one of the most difficult modes to maintain, as a human. To sustain a joyous outlook is problematic when facing life's daily challenges and navigating your way through emotional turmoil. Joy is an outreach of 'love' and is a by-product of giving and receiving that energy. When humans were first created by superior intelligent beings, they were meant to serve as slaves, contending with daily strife on a lower, base level of emotions. Joy and revelling in exulted happiness was not part of the intended agenda. That is why people find it difficult to embrace and sustain joy because, embedded in their DNA is the default of guilt and self-deprecation as a punishment for being happy."

I understand that insecurity very well. I often feel guilty for being happy, fearing it will be taken away from me. Mimi understands my dilemma and continues:

"Joy, love and happiness are powerful emotions which cut through the negative wiring in your DNA. The more you allow yourself to be happy, the more you destroy the destructive elements preventing you from being your true self and living in a state of true love which is your real legacy. I want to show you something. It isn't a place, it is a state of being."

She bends her head low so that we are face to face and I am lost in the wonder of her eyes which gleam like verdant green meadows swimming with yellow poppies. She knows I am always a little nervous to climb on her back but telepathically she assures me and gives me confidence to reach up and sit behind her neck with my arms clutching her scaly throat. The take- off is gentle and smooth as we glide upwards into the ionosphere where, beyond Earth, the atmosphere is like a multi-layered cake which we do not cut through, but rather exit sideways through a black rotating tunnel where neon flashes of lightening streaks flare out like electric tentacles. Ultra-violet, iridescent rays burn through the blackness as microscopic particles explode into tiny ashes of golden dust. Travelling beyond the speed of light we are timeless as the cosmos dances around us. I hear the chuckling laughter of a child, growing louder and louder until I am inside the sound, reverberating as one vibration. All my senses tingle with joy and innocent delight as I become the laughter which expands and grows into a massive upsurge of spontaneous, roaring, cachinnation and I am drenched, saturated, flooded, swamped in sheer joy until I am exhausted. It is like being tickled beyond endurance.

Suddenly we are back in Mimi's magical forest and I lie down in the heavenly grass laughing and laughing until all is calm. Mimi watches like a protective Mother and when I am at rest she whispers:

"Happiness is a state of being. No matter what is causing you pain, you must remember that joy is the greater warrior, for sooner or later happiness will win through, if you allow it. Try to find joy in all that you do and it will find you and reward you."

I close my eyes and she fades. I am back on my decking in my little cabin watching the sun sink slowly behind the trees weaving a golden pathway to the twilight temple where the day's gilded rays meet the edge of the evening. Freddie, my canine friend sits loyally beside me and together we watch my tiny solar lights spring into action changing colour in random sequences, illuminating my flowers and plants in a fairyland halo of shimmering magic. My two faithful cats watch superciliously from the window, seated royally at my desk, deigning to share the twilight embers, folding into the black night. In this moment I am happy and lucky to know love and be loved, which can never die – just as death is not the end, it is the beginning of another adventure, where we will meet again.

9 781835 380840